I0633512

RESET

PAOLO
PERGOLA

 Sagging
Meniscus

© 2021 by Paolo Pergola

All Rights Reserved.

Set in Adobe Garamond Pro with LaTeX.

ISBN: 978-1-952386-12-1 (paperback)
ISBN: 978-1-952386-13-8 (ebook)
Library of Congress Control Number: 2021942452

Sagging Meniscus Press
Montclair, New Jersey
saggingmeniscus.com

Contents

RESET

Like he does every morning

Like he does every morning, Dr. Braglia came to check the patients at nine o'clock today. That guy is not a doctor, he is a Swiss watch. And today was the day they were removing the cast from my right arm, so now I can write. I am still struggling, my arm still hurts, but I can write.

I've been in bed for three months now in this hospital room, orthopedic ward, next to Marshal Danovaro on one side, the left, and the kid Lorenzo, on the other, that is, the right. This is what it is about, a hospital room, its smells and dim noises, and other noises that sometimes come from the outside like clandestine aliens. And me, in the middle of this room for three full months, January, February and March.

This morning I also had a long discussion with Dr. Broglia, I just asked him if it would be possible to do a brain transplant. He didn't take it well, almost as if I asked him something personal, and then he told me, Why do you need a brain transplant? I replied that it wasn't like I really wanted to have my brain transplanted, I just wanted to know if it was possible at all, nowadays everything can be transplanted, hands have been transplanted, a face, hundreds of hearts transplanted, and kidneys, livers, pretty much everything, and therefore I was wondering if brains could also be transplanted. But Dr. Braglia told me, I'm not falling for it, Pardini, I know you by now, what are you getting at? What's wrong with your brain? It's too full, I told him, I would love to have an empty one. If you have an empty brain available, I would gladly exchange it with mine. Pardini, Pardini, you like to joke around too much, Dr. Bruglia told me, I don't have that much time to waste. Just try to get better, you'll see, your head will get better on its own.

Maybe Dr. Bruglia is right. I've been here for three months, I got hit real bad, the only thing I remember is that I was walking by the side of a state road in the evening, and then *boom*. Nothing else. They found me in a ditch the next morning, those town employees who come to pick up the cats hit by cars repeatedly, so much that they end up looking like doormats. I ended up in a ditch, but I was still alive. They brought me here with multiple fractures, that is, it was easier to say what wasn't broken, I was told, my nose and my left hand. All the other bones were pretty much broken.

Even my head was hit badly. At first, I didn't remember anything at all. One day a woman came into my room, took my hand, the left one, and looked at me. It was nice. I didn't know who she was, but isn't that always the case? Now that my memory has come back, and I know that that woman was my wife, now—I wonder—but wasn't it better before, when I didn't know who she was, than now, now that I think I know who she is?

What do I know now? Nothing. First, small fragments of memory came back to me, then whole pieces, then everything, now I remember everything, I know everything, but what do I know, really? Nothing. When you look at it, I only know what I knew right after the accident. Nothing. Why didn't I stay there, at that level of unconsciousness, where a strange woman came to see me and held my hand?

Now Dr. Brilla says that I remember virtually everything, now I'm almost back to normal, he also did a test on me and I got a very high score. Too bad. My only hope would be a brain transplant, with a brain that is empty though. I couldn't care less for a full or an almost-full brain. Not even half full. It should be an empty brain, and then I would be very careful not to fill it.

Because I was doing quite well when I was completely empty inside. I looked at people and they all looked the same. I wasn't even wondering, Is this guy here, lying on a bed next to mine, one of my old friends? As it turned out, that was the Marshal. Then my memory came back to me, and I recognized my family, my friends, and those I didn't recognize it was because I didn't know them. This I can understand. But couldn't it be that experience gives you a wrong image of things around you?

People come to see me

People come to see me sometimes, in the morning, from eleven to noon, or in the evening, from seven to eight o'clock. My mother, for example. And my wife Karin. They come here, they talk. I don't have much to say. Sometimes I answer their questions. I look at them and I think that they are my mother and my wife, but it's also possible that somebody, while I was unconscious in the ditch, has gotten me a mother and a wife who I didn't have before, or had other ones, and then this somebody injected the memory of this mother and this wife into my brain, and therefore I recognize them as such now, but something tells me that I'm not so sure any more. Because I remember well that day, when a woman I didn't know came into my room and took my hand. I didn't know her, but she was my wife, as it turned out, because of the memory they injected in me. But nobody has removed the memory of the day she came into my room and I didn't know her. I remember quite well that I didn't know her. Therefore, one could say that there are two parallel lines of thought. According to the first one, I didn't know my wife, and then I remembered who she was (because of the injection). The second line of thought is about remembering that I didn't know who she was at the time. And often, in my head, this second line of thought takes over.

My mother always tells me, When you get out . . . She tells me, When you get out, we'll go to the beach house . . . When you get out you'll have to do physiotherapy, I know a great physiotherapist . . . When you get out we'll have a nice dinner at the restaurant . . . When you get out I'll show you how I've redecorated the living room . . .

I don't know when I will get out of here. Actually, I'm not even sure I want to get out. Here, I can keep everything under control. During the day I focus my attention on the ceiling. With my eyes, I travel through the stains on the ceiling, I go for long walks between one stain and the other. At night, I sleep.

I also remembered that I am a biologist. I was a biologist. When I had my accident, I had just started writing a research project together with Corrado Malvezzi, a colleague of mine, about the effect of hypoxia—the lack of oxygen dissolved in the water—on fish. Malvezzi, he also comes to visit me every now and then. The first time he stopped by was when my memory had just come back. He never showed up before then. The project on hypoxia, he said, do you remember that? Yes, I told him. Well, that project, it's due in fifteen days, would you be able to write your part, huh, what do you say, would you be able to make it?

I remember the project on hypoxia, I told him, yes, I remember it, but no, I don't think I'll be able to write my part. I wouldn't even know where to start. But you've already started, Malvezzi told me, don't you remember, you've already written four or five pages. I don't know what else I could write, I told him. Well, Malvezzi said, just pick up from where you left off, you were writing about the protocols necessary to establish the oxygen thresholds, etcetera, etcetera . . . I wouldn't know what to make of it, I said. But there is nothing to be made, Malvezzi said, and then, I will be there to help you, c'mon . . . I'm sorry, I don't know how to write the project on hypoxia any more, I told him, there's nothing you can do about it, I'm sorry . . . listen, would you mind opening the window just a little bit?

Malvezzi opened the window and then left. He has come back several times. Including today. He always starts out with a different topic, today he even asked me if I had watched a Juventus match. I didn't watch the Juventus match, I slept. So you didn't know that Juventus lost? I didn't know that Juventus lost, nope, I had no idea. Yeah, said Malvezzi, who is a Juventus fan, I told you we should change coaches, if we keep going this way we won't get anywhere. Uh-huh, I replied.

Slowly Malvezzi veered the topic of conversation from soccer to other hobbies, he told me about his tennis games with another colleague, Schifano, and about beating him every single time—that is, Malvezzi beats Schifano—When you get out of here, we'll play a double's match, he told me, what d'you say? I don't know, I don't play tennis. C'mon you always say that, I bet you're pretty good. No, Corrado, I've never played tennis, and then I'm not going to get out of here. What are you talking about, Lapo, c'mon, you'll be out in a month. Nope, I don't think so, I told him, I really do not think so.

Finally, after talking about tennis, or about any other sport for that matter, he always ends up talking about the project. You know, he told me, Schifano, the other day, after tennis, we went for a beer. Uh-huh, I told him. Well, as it turns out, Schifano, he's going to help us out with the project, what d'you say, isn't that a good idea? Good idea, I told him, good idea. He'll write your part and then he can send it to you via email so that you can edit it, what d'you say? I don't know, what can I edit, there's nothing to edit, I told him. C'mon, Lapo, he said, you'll read it, and then you'll fix it up, he doesn't have your experience, with all the nice work you've done over the years etcetera etcetera . . . Please drop it, I told him, I won't read Schifano's part, I told him, there's nothing you can do about it, sorry, and then, would you mind opening the window just a little bit?

He was here for a whole hour, I had to give in. I said he could tell Schifano to send me the project via email, otherwise he would not have left my room. I'm pretty sure he'll come back sooner or later. I don't really think that Malvezzi hopes that I will start working on the project. He comes here just to spend some time, comes to see me, bug me a little bit, see what happens. And that's how he spends his free time, I guess.

Marshal Danovaro, on the other hand

Marshal Danovaro, on the other hand, watched the Juventus game on his little desk television. Geez, he tells me, your colleague's right, Juventus, I mean, they ought to change their coach! Uh-huh, I answer. Don't you like soccer? he asks me. I don't know, I tell him, in the darkest moments of my life I did watch a few games, but when I was doing well, no, I didn't care much about football. And now? he asks me, which was kind of like asking me how it's going, whether I'm having one of the darkest moments or if I'm okay.

I wouldn't mind watching a game every now and then, I tell him. Tomorrow there's a Rome game, he says, waiting for my comment. The Rome team, y'know, he insists, not those Juventus types. Whaddaya think, you wanna watch it together? Sure thing, I tell him, sure thing. Meanwhile, in the other bed, Lorenzo the kid continues beating his fingertips on his mini laptop while playing one of his thousands of video games. He's doin' the click-click-click, as the Marshal says.

C'mon Lorenzo, says the Marshal, whaddaya say if we watch the Rome game tonight, you gonna be one of us? Hey you, can you hear me, Lorenzo? Lorenzo raises his head from the video game head and says, What game? Whaddaya mean, what game? The Rome game, c'mon, I told ya, Rome is playing, they are all gonna be there, even the captain. What time is it going to be? asks Lorenzo. How am I supposed to know? replies Marshal Danovaro. I have no freaking idea, but what d'ya care? What, you got somethin' better to do, ha? No, just to know, says Lorenzo. Dear God, Lorenzo, what have we gotta do? There's nothing to do here, we're stuck, at least we can watch a friggin' soccer game, for Chrissakes.

Lorenzo doesn't give a damn about the game, but he doesn't say it. He spends about ten hours a day playing with that gizmo, sucked in by video games. The Marshal, on the other hand, is getting ready for the big game. He goes on and on about Totti, the team's captain, and the line defense, there's one with three players, and there's another one with four players, and apparently one is better than the other. I pretend to listen to him a little bit, though my head is spinning. I envy Lorenzo who is hiding behind his video games. Then finally the Marshal falls asleep.

I don't even know what time it is. The hours here, what does it matter? The only events are a few visits, and meals. Occasionally some doctors or nurses. (And the Rome game, c'mon.)

Or else, I play with my memories, now that they have all come back together, like so many messenger pigeons on their way home. Who knows where they went when I had lost them. Who knows if there is a place where lost memories end up, forgotten things, which as far as existence goes, they do exist, even if they are no longer in anyone's mind, they must be somewhere, they cannot disappear.

Now my memories are back, in a random order. Scenes from when I was a child, mixed in with things that happened to me last year, the *before* and the *after* reshuffled, and the faces, the voices, all scattered here and there. There's a day that often comes to my mind, in slightly different versions. That day when I was in second grade, and a girl fainted during the mid-morning break. Our teacher wasn't there, so all the kids were kind of scared. Finally, a janitor showed up and called an ambulance. It was nothing serious, perhaps the girl had skipped breakfast and was having a sugar low. I started to fantasize that, one day, perhaps Caterina Magri, the girl who was always sitting in the front row wearing jeans with colored patches, would have skipped breakfast, and would faint during the mid-morning break. But this time I would be ready to jump out of the first-floor window and I would run to the nearby hospital and I would become a hero.

I would become a hero, running like a crazy hero. I fantasized about the different shortcuts that I could have taken, from the school to the hospital, through the park, or through the arcades. I figured that running through the park would be the best choice, the park must be kind of empty at that hour, during our mid-morning break. But I wasn't sure, because I had never been to the park during our mid-morning break. I was picturing myself running like crazy, that was the best part of the whole scene. Jumping from the first floor wasn't that bad either, but perhaps a little too dramatic. Besides, I wasn't that good at jumping off the first floor. In fact, I had never even tried. I preferred to focus on the running bit. I was running to save Caterina Magri who fainted because of a skipped breakfast. All I needed was for her to skip breakfast, and I would become a hero. It didn't seem so unlikely. Every morning I looked at her closely to try to figure out if by chance she had skipped breakfast. But it wasn't easy to tell, at a glance. To make things worse, she was always sitting in the first row, on the other side of the classroom, it was hard to see anything.

She was always so full of energy, Caterina Magri. I don't know if she ever skipped breakfast. And even if she had skipped it, maybe she wouldn't have fainted. As a matter of fact, she never fainted. For four years, from first to fourth grade, she never fainted. To be honest, I only checked how she was doing starting from second grade, because that was when that other girl fainted, and had somehow offered me the key to get to Caterina Magri. Who, however, never fainted. At least, she didn't until the end of the fourth grade. After that, I don't know, because for my fifth grade my family moved to another city and I ended up in a class where instead of fainting, the boys punched each other during the mid-morning break.

After so many years, every now and then I found myself thinking about my run through the half-empty park and about a fainting Caterina Magri whom I saved. And this thought was mixed with all the other things I remembered about all those years, on which I was sitting, and each was the result of something that had happened and other things that had not happened to me but that I had imagined myself, and so they too, in a way, had happened to me. And I asked myself: Why? As for Caterina Magri, I now figured out, rationally, that she had not fainted because she must have had her breakfast every single morning. But all the other things that had happened to me, how could they be explained?

I don't want to have anything to do with all these things that happened to me anymore. I would like to take advantage of the fact that I had lost my memory of all these things and I was doing great. Well, maybe not that great, but at least I wasn't doing so bad. But now, now that all these things have come back to me, I feel this weight that pulls me down. That's when I'd rather concentrate on that short period in which I had forgotten everything and then, slowly, things came back to the surface, in a random order. And one of the first things that had surfaced from my sunken memory was my run to save Caterina Magri.

At times it's not really memories

At times it's not really memories, but a series of images, that comes to me. Images that spin in my head while I am half asleep, knocked out by medicines. It's like I am floating up in the air, or in the water. Actually, this feeling of being in the water happens to me quite often these days. I am in the water, surrounded by other fish, because I am also one of them in these images. I am lagging behind, at the very back of a huge school of sardines that are swimming slowly along the coast. I notice that there are some fishing lines dropped into the water. Almost all of us avoid them, but every now and then a fish gets caught.

What a loser, I think, we all know that's a hook, and that's a line. Well, I guess that even knowing that, some of these fish cannot help but go for a bite, it's instinctive, you can see from the fishy looks they give us, the survivors, while the lines pull them up, out of the water.

We are all sorry to see our buddies getting caught every now and then, but we continue to swim undeterred. Maybe I ended up in a fish school during their migratory season? It looks like it, given that they swim in a straight line, without any detours. Next to me, my neighbors send me silvery flashes with scales, glitters that maybe I should interpret somehow. The feeling of swimming is quite pleasant, like gliding away effortless. And the pain that I felt in my legs become less intense, more like a background noise.

Even the Marshal's snoring noise, the ticking on Lorenzo's computer and the light of the room fade into the sea depths. I let myself be carried away by the vortices that the fish in front of me create. The school gets bigger and bigger, other fish join us from right and left. But now there are too many of us, I start to run out of oxygen, the fish in front of me consume all the oxygen and there is no more left for those of us who are behind. We thought we could get away with it, taking advantage of the trails of those in front. But no, there is a downside, we are screwed, and now we are too far behind, there is no way to reach the front of the school, that's it, we have to let go of the school. And it is at this point that I realize I am in a hospital bed, with the lights of a room hanging from the ceiling, and next to me, instead of two sardines, Lorenzo is on one side, the Marshal on the other.

Then there's Karin, the woman who came one day

Then there's Karin, the woman who came one day to hold my hand and I didn't know who she was, and it turned out she was my wife. There she was again, she came back today, and instead of holding my hand, she said, I brought you your laptop. What am I supposed to do with it? I asked her. You can work on it, or write to friends, do whatever you want with it, she replied.

She started to put the computer on my lap, then she thought better of it, she must have realized that my legs are still broken. So, in the end, she didn't lay the computer on my lap, she looked around then she placed it on the table on my left. Here you go, she said. I don't know if I will use it, I told her. Do as you like, she replied. Are all my files in there? I asked her. All your files are in there, she replied, I haven't touched anything.

I'd prefer an empty computer, I told her. She didn't reply. Sometimes Karin is very good at ignoring me. So, I took the computer in my hands. I shook it a little, as if to empty it physically. Karin looked out the window and said, You know, people ask me about you, how you are . . . what I'm trying to say is that maybe you could get on Facebook so that people see how you are, how you progress. How I progress? Yes, I mean, like when they changed the cast on your leg, or when your memory came back, things like that would be nice to show your friends on Facebook. Right, I told her.

I didn't manage to say anything else. I thought of many things to say, but then I only came out with *Right*. Maybe in twenty years it will seem normal to everyone to be on Facebook, as happened with the phone. But in my case, I don't know why, I just can't communicate without a direct interlocutor. Of course, it would be easier, you write a few lines, you post a picture so that all of your friends and acquaintances can see it. It's a pretty efficient system, much easier than just calling people one by one, or sending a personalized email message to everyone. It's as if from the segments that link two people we had moved to the planes, or rather, to three dimensions, to the spheres. And the person who writes or posts a bunch of photos on Facebook would be the center of the sphere, from which everything one has to say or to show irradiates. The users of this system, that is, your Facebook friends, are inside the sphere, and each one of them has his or her own sphere, so a whole world comes out of this, made of these spheres that overlap and intersect.

I much prefer segments to spheres. Even in the past, as a child, or as a boy, basically as far as I can remember, I never managed to cope with being in a group. Meeting people one by one is fine, I can talk and listen, I can make friends this way. On the other hand, if there are four or five of us, there are too many tangles and I don't know what to do any more, usually I just shut up. My impression was that if you interacted with someone as a single person, even bullies from school, if you happened to bump into them when they were alone, like on a bus, you could chat them up. It may not always be this way, but I had this idea, and at school I was friendly with everyone, but one at a time, not all together. And some of these friends hated each other, so now I am not sure how it would work to have them all on the same Facebook page.

I'm not interested in efficiency and functionality. I eat, sleep, read, speak unwillingly, remember. In a little while, maybe I'll even stop talking. I don't have a fixed plan. Perhaps I will keep talking to people, especially if they come to see me one at a time. From this point of view, the hospital mainly offers interactions of this type.

I could hear Karin who was still talking about Facebook. She was saying that she is on Facebook and that she posts photos for her friends and her New Zealand family. Karin is from New Zealand. She said that when she travels, she always posts the photos of her trip on Facebook. And she also writes down the dates, so that people know where she is, and when.

I'm right here, I told her, it's easy to know where I am, I'm right here. And I don't take photos. But you made some progress, she told me, you could post it on Facebook. I don't make any progress, I told her, I don't seem to be making any progress. In fact, perhaps I regressed a little, especially when I regained my memory. I think I was doing much better before, and in any case now that I am resetting my brain, I will be very careful not to fill it up with new things.

Don't be silly, she said, I'm not silly, I told her, I just don't seem to be making progress. Karin looked at me, What are you looking at? I asked her. Nothing, she said, it's that we always end up fighting over anything. We're not fighting, I told her, why, were we fighting? I don't know, she said, you have become so idle. I'm not idle, I'm recovering. You're idly recovering, everyone has figured it out, even Malvezzi, she said. Malvezzi, what does Malvezzi have to do with it? I said. I bumped into him the other day at the supermarket, said Karin. Why did you bump into Malvezzi? I didn't bump into him on purpose, he was there, I said hello and he asked me about you, said Karin. And did he tell you I am idle? No, no, he didn't say *idle*, I mean, he said that he asked you for some help on some work-related stuff but you don't want to help him, she said. Malvezzi can go to hell, as far as I am concerned, I said. Well, I didn't really want to talk about Malvezzi, she said, you see how we always fight?

And then we went on like this for a while. It was much better when I didn't remember who Karin was, I didn't even know her name, she was just the woman who held my hand while I was all dazed by the sedatives and I watched her holding my hand. If I concentrate and think about it, I see the scene of this woman who comes into my room and takes my left hand, I feel her hand, the little hills and valleys of her hand against my little hills and valleys and it almost seems like they fit together.

Come to think of it, Malvezzi

Come to think of it, Malvezzi, why the hell would he start talking to Karin at all? Malvezzi, that man, is a threat to society. I remember the feeling of anguish when I was at work and he used to come into my office without knocking. I remember this very well. I remember that as soon as he came into the office, my cells, not only my liver cells and my neurons, but all of them, even the epithelial ones lining the intestine, all my cells started to secrete bile. I felt like shrinking while he placed himself right there, in front of me, and there was no way to kick him out.

Malvezzi would just come into my office, he always wanted a little help with something, but he never got straight to the point.

First, he would talk about his children, or about soccer, about anything. Then he would ask for some help with a translation, or with a plane ticket, or anything else that any adult can do and that Malvezzi probably knew how to do but would never have done unless the entire human population had become extinct. And in that case, then, whatever it was that he wanted to do would no longer make sense.

This is how it usually started out. Malvezzi was working on something, like writing a report or a project. At some point he would ask me for a little help, so I helped him, and slowly it turned out that everything was on me. He avoided all possible tasks. If there was a meeting for that project, he did not attend it, if there was someone to call, he disappeared. Eventually, when the project or report was finished, he magically reappeared, just to put his signature on it. At this point, the project went back to being *his* project again, after I wrote it, or after anyone else wrote it, anyone who had fallen for Malvezzi's trickery that surrounded you and left you no way out.

Malvezzi is a good enough reason to make me want to stay here in this hospital. One day I may have a half-hearted desire to breathe a little fresh air, and there will be the image of Malvezzi, that will be enough to immediately appease any desire for me to get out of here. The thought that Malvezzi's presence, his proximity, once outside, could affect me, could make me be like him, freezes my legs and nails me down to this bed.

Not to mention when he starts talking about this and that, like when he is jealous of a colleague or someone else. I have to listen to him because he stands right there in front of my door. And so he drags me into his vortex of malice, his nasty comments about this and that, which boil down to his desire to prevail. Social climbing has never interested me, and now that I'm out, that is, here in this hospital, now I don't even climb anymore, I don't race with anyone, Malvezzi can also lap me, I'm here, sitting still. I see myself as if I were in an Olympic stadium, everybody is running and I was running too, but now I have stopped, I have moved to the side of the four-hundred meter track, and I am sitting on the grass.

Today it occurred to me

Today it occurred to me that, in addition to saving Caterina Magri who had fainted during our mid-morning break, as a young boy I dreamed that I would become a movie director when I was grown up. It must have happened in middle school, that is, a few years after not having saved Caterina Magri, when I came up with this idea. I dreamed of becoming a movie director, of becoming quite famous, and then shooting the movie I had always dreamed of, a movie filmed and produced by myself. I would have called this self-produced and self-filmed movie "Closed Today". I remember that it didn't matter what the movie was going to be about, I mean, it could have been a western with fistfights and pistols, a kind of remake of Sergio Leone's films and it would have been just fine. It could also have been a comedy, a thriller, or even a thriller comedy, that would have been alright. The important thing was not the content, but the title: "Closed Today".

And then I fantasized about what the newspapers would write on their list of today's movies—at the Odeon in Milan, surely there must be an Odeon theater in Milan, I imagined, "Odeon: Rambo 18", at the Central "Central: Dumb and

Dumber", and so on. Finally, at Ariston, "Ariston: Closed Today". Nobody would go to the Ariston on a day off. The Ariston
would be empty on that day. All the theaters with my movie
would be empty. Hundreds of protest letters from cinema owners.

My movie would have been a major failure, at first. Until, by
dint of talking about it, people would have gotten used to the
idea of a movie entitled "Closed Today", indeed, they would be
curious, how's this movie? . . . with such a funny title . . . let's go
see it. At that point, people could end up going to a movie theater on a day when the theater really was closed. And so, more
stacks of letters, this time from the consumer associations. Cine-
mas would have to figure out another way of telling people they
were closed, such as "No Movies Today". "No Movies Today"
would then be a perfect title, for the sequel to my film "Closed
Today".

Come to think of it though, being a movie director is a bit
complicated. Especially now, with all my broken bones, and I'm
stuck at the hospital. Not to mention that I have no intention of
getting out. Writing a book, on the other hand, would be much
easier. For the title, I could use the same principle as "Closed
Today".

This is what I was thinking about, this morning. I wanted
to find the book-equivalent of the movie title I had thought of
when I was a kid. Luckily, Karin brought me a computer, so I
ended up using it. I found a bookstore website. I typed a few
random letters into the search engine, like Asdasdf. Clearly it
wasn't that random after all, because the site found several books,
none titled Asdasdf, nor written by some Asdasdf writer, but
written by writers whose names were almost Asdasdf. Like the

time I went to a bookstore to buy Dino Campana's *Canti Orfici*, and the bookseller told me they didn't have it in stock, but there was a book by Campanella if it might interest me. Anyways, as for Asdasdf, since it wasn't random enough, I improved it a bit, I called it Asdasdfasaddadsads. This worked for my research. With Asdasdfasaddadsads, the website tells me:—*Your search produced no results—Please try again by entering a new word to search for—*. A bit too long for a title. I try on another website. Here, for Asdasdfasaddadsads the website replies: *No title found*. There you have it.

You go to a bookstore, you look for a book, then you go to the counter and say I don't remember the title, what was it? *In Search of a Title*, something like that, but I do remember the author, it's so-and-so. The bookseller looks it up on her computer, and all she gets is *No Title Found*. I'm sorry, sir, but there is no title by that author. Out of curiosity, I also checked on my computer to see what comes up if one looks for *No Title found*, on that bookstore website. If you look for *No Title found*, you get *No Title Found*.

But today I don't really want to write a book entitled *No Title Found*. I would rather write a book that has no title and no words. And without pages or a cover. I would like empty nothingness, maybe even without its container.

Today my mother came by

Today my mother came by and updated me on her top ten hits. Her top ten hits look like this: in tenth place, for a couple of months, there is her car which has the muffler that's falling apart, the muffler is falling apart so she took the car to the Vicar who is not a priest but a mechanic whose name is Vicar, and the Vicar told her, But ma'am, you should change your car, it's now ten years old! But I don't want to change it, my mom tells me, You know that Dad bought it before he left me for that woman, but even if he's gone I don't want to change my car, and anyways why did he leave me? [in ninth place, in the ranking for three years], I bet it's because he was bored at work, that woman has nothing to do with it, she's even kind of ugly, with her double chin and all, the problem was that he was bored at work, and I should have figured it out, I should have entertained him more, we should have travelled together more, gone out in the evenings, he always said he wanted to travel, instead I stayed at home knitting all the time and he was bored, we should have travelled around the world but we didn't, that's why he fled to Buenos Aires with that woman, she's even part Argentinian, did you know?—I know, I know—Anyways, he doesn't really like her, I know your father quite well, he just wanted to go to Argentina, or maybe Argentina isn't the problem, all he wanted was a bit of a change, who wouldn't want a bit of a change? I would like a bit of a change too . . . sure . . . but I don't mean the car, and then all these modern cars have an expression that I don't like at all, they all look kind of aggressive, with those futuristic lights and they're too big anyways, how can people drive such huge cars? How can they do that? The thing is that I don't want to change the car, I even told Simone [my brother], I don't want to change it, I told him, Simone, he's so busy, now he has made up his mind to buy me a new car, poor thing, Simone, he has to go to Munich every single week . . .

In eighth place, for several weeks, there is Simone who *has* to go to Munich every single week. Why don't you give him a call one of these days? my mother asks me. And what happened to your cell phone? I don't have it anymore, I tell her, it broke when I had my accident, don't you remember? You're right, she says, I forgot, so I'll bring you a new one. As you wish, Mom. I'll bring you a new one, don't you worry, so that you can call Simone who has to go to Munich every week, since they closed their Milan office, did you hear about that?—I heard, I heard ... —Right, so now he *has* to go to Munich, why don't you call him one of these days, I'll bring you a new cell phone, so you also call Uncle Beppe, did you hear about his operation? [in seventh place, in the ranking for two weeks], you should call him too, now that he's better, they sent him home, now he's better, but it was pretty tough, you know, they practically operated on him twice, one operation after the other, he was in the operating room for six full hours, you should give him a call, I'm sure he'd appreciate it.

My mom reels off the whole top ten hits, including the new entries, like the magnolia that is about to fall down in the garden, then the water bills that she has to pay like everybody else in her condo, even if she lives on her own, now that my father is gone (with that ugly woman and her double chin). Every now and again I actually listen to her, then she asks me about me, [I myself have been in the ranking for three months, that is, since I had the accident], how am I—I'm fine Mom—Great, so they'll let you out?—I don't know Mom, I don't know, and to tell you the truth, I don't really want get out—Stop that nonsense, she says, of course you want to get out [my mother knows *exactly* what I do and don't want to do].

Finally, she leaves, she has to go because there is a condo meeting even if she doesn't want to go, she says. This thing of the top ten hits, I have it too, I got it from my mother. Or, rather, I *had* it, before the accident, because when I got here I was pretty much done with this top ten thing. But before my accident, I always had a nice little list of my top ten hits, with things like the project with Malvezzi, my problems with Karin, my bills, my car to be fixed, my chronic back pain. Funny how my chronic back pain was gone as soon as I got to the hospital, it must have been because they stuffed me up with pain killers especially at the beginning, with so many broken bones. In the end my back pain was gone, just like that, and so were my top ten hits.

At first, I wasn't aware of having changed, I simply didn't remember a thing, it was like I had been completely reset, as if all the garbage in my brain had been cleaned out. Then I started to remember everything, including the top ten hits. Only now it's not affecting me any longer, now I see it as the top ten hits of another person who isn't me. I even remember clearly what was in the top ten hits before the accident, sometimes I dare venture to review the details of all the rankings, since now I am immune because of the accident. Sometimes my mother takes it upon herself to remind me of my top ten hits, since part of my old top ten hits was the same as hers. For example, I too, when my father left us, started thinking about all the things we should have done to avoid his departure. I remember that sometimes I would see him in my dreams and then I thought about it all day.

Instead, now I picture him on the streets of Buenos Aires feeding the pigeons. There was this old black and white photo that made a big impression on me as a child, it was not a photo of my father, but of a distant grandson of my mother's, who was standing in a square in Buenos Aires with a couple of pigeons on his arm, and he was feeding them. I had never had a pigeon land on my arm and it seemed to me a magical thing, something that perhaps happened only in Buenos Aires. Since then, I have always associated Buenos Aires with pigeons, so when my father left us, I was sure he would go around the squares of Buenos Aires to feed the pigeons.

He doesn't get in touch with us all that often, my father. Only on special occasions like for Christmas and for some birthdays. He comes to Italy a couple of weeks in the summer, then he comes to see us and we have dinner together. He has an email address but hardly ever uses it. He has no phone. A few days after the accident, he sent me a telegram saying *Heard of the accidente. Get well soon. Dad.* My mother brought it to me in a yellow envelope. I left it there on the nightstand for a few days. When I opened it, I read it several times, looking between the lines in Spanish of the Correos Argentinos header to see if by chance there wasn't some other encrypted information left by my father. I was picturing my father dictating the text to an Argentine operator. I pictured my father in a telephone booth while dictating *Heard of the accident*, and the operator who wrote *accidente*. Meanwhile my father was looking at the pigeons from the telephone booth in the Plaza de Mayo. And then he would add, Get well soon, which could be seen like some kind of order, *Make sure to get well soon*, or a way of reassuring me, *Don't worry, you'll get well soon*. But in my father's case it was probably neither, getting well soon was simply a consequence of the accident that led to a recovery that, in a relative sense, would have happened soon. My father is not the kind of guy who would let people see what's in his mind. Actually, there is nothing to see in his case. When people talk, they always tend to interpret. My father, on the other hand, he means only that very thing, there is never any hidden meaning attached to what he says. As far as talking goes, he is not much of a talker. He speaks slowly, and not much, my father. Sometimes, as I recall, he answers questions with a yes or a no but doesn't tend to dwell much on the details.

My brother Marco came to see me this morning

My brother Marco came to see me this morning. He brought his eleven-year-old daughter Luisa along. Marco is a doctor, so at some point he left the room to look for Dr. Brilla. He left Luisa with me, and she wanted to ask me something. She wanted to ask me if I could answer some questions so that she could write it down on my eco-report card. I have no idea what an eco-report card is, and I didn't know I had one, I tell her. Children never know what you know or what you don't know. Sometimes they explain things that are obvious to everyone, but they don't know that, and other times they don't explain things you've never heard of, but there is no way for them to know that. Luisa explains to me what an eco-report card is, it's a report card that is made for adults in the family, like you Uncle Lapo, she tells me. Of course, I say, and she goes on with the explanation, Mrs. Monica gave it to us, first we have to ask the adults all the questions, then we write down their answers and their scores, that's how you do the eco-report card. I get it, I tell her, and what are the questions? They are all questions about recycling, like when you put your garbage in different bags, one for glass, one for plastic, that's how you recycle, but I can't tell you more because otherwise I will help you too much, she tells me. Of course, I tell her, then go ahead, ask me the questions. Are you ready? she asks me.

I'm ready. Luisa asks me six or seven questions together with three possible answers, I just have to choose answer a, b or c. Among the answers there is always one that is kind of funny, like, Where are you supposed to put glass? Just throw it on the ground to break it into a thousand pieces. Luisa tries to stay serious, reads the three answers and then tells me, So, uncle Lapo, is it a, b, or c? I try to remember the intricate mechanisms of recycling. Finding the ridiculous answer is easy but choosing between the other two is not that easy. And although in some cases it's easy, I still think about it a bit, so that I can look at Luisa's expression while she's holding her pencil in her right hand and my eco-report card in her left hand. After each question, Luisa puts a mark on my eco-report card and raises her eyebrows, as if she found out if my answer was correct or not only at that point.

You did well, uncle Lapo, she tells me at the end, you got all the right answers. And now? I ask her. Now you have to sign here, and she hands me my eco-report card, here, where it says *Signature of the adult,* and so I sign. Luisa checks my signature, then tells me, Now I put your eco-report card together with Dad's and Mom's and Aunt Karin's reports and I give them to Mrs. Monica. Miss-Harmonica? I ask her. No, Mrs. Monica, she says. Ah, I thought you said Miss-Harmonica, I say.

Hey, I tell her, what if we call her Miss-Harmonica, it could be like our secret code, what do you think? Sure! yes, she says, and what about the other ones? The other ones? I ask. Yes, the other teachers, Luisa says, what should we call them? You are right, we need a code for them too, of course, what are these other teachers' names? So, there's Mrs. Selena, who does mathematics . . . Okay, we can call her Misscellanea, then. Then there's Mrs. Lidia . . . That's easy, we'll call her Missleading. And then there's Mrs. Teresa. Me-stress-you, I tell her. So, there's Miss-harmonica, then . . . Misscellanea, I suggest. So, Miss-harmonica, Misscellanea, Missleading and Me-stress-you, right? Quite right, I tell her. So tomorrow I'll give your eco-report card to Miss-Harmonica . . . Okay, I say. And tomorrow . . . tomorrow . . . for the first two hours we have Missleading, says Luisa, and then Miss-Harmonica. On Friday we have Misscellanea first, and then Me-stress-you.

Meanwhile Marco comes back, and tells me, Hey Lapo, so it looks like you're doing better now, Braglia told me. As far as doing, I'm not really doing anything, I tell him. He also told me that sometimes you talk a bit oddly. Like what? I mean, he told me that you asked him about a brain transplant, what was that about? Were you making fun of him? No, no way, I wasn't, I just wanted to know if it was possible, my brain still feels too full, I was much better off when I had forgotten everything, I felt lighter. I think you're full of shit, Lapo, why don't you just focus on getting better now, you'll see, everything will be fine by the time you get out. That's exactly my point, I tell him, I don't want to get out, I really don't. Okay, but you cannot go on like this, says Marco, when you're well, you'll be sent home, and you'll also have to go back to work. It's true, holy shingles, I hadn't thought of that. At this point Marco says goodbye, Luisa sends me a kiss, and they leave. Marco is right. I had not thought about that. When I get better physically they will send me home and I will have to go back to work. I had left the game, it seemed pretty easy, I certainly didn't do it on purpose, and it was also kind of painful, but now I don't want to get back into the game.

Now that I'm stuck here, I've discovered the power of thinking, the beauty of thinking. I play with all the memories that emerge together, I pick one up and I look at it carefully, I turn it over and over, I remember it, I tell it to myself, and then I take another one and so on, I never get bored, I don't need to move around. It would be an unnecessary effort, an effort that frightens me, it weighs on me just thinking about it, it's an effort that I don't see the point of. I'm here, I'm not expecting anything, except my collection of memories. The rest, whatever it is that I could be doing, would be nothing but bad copies of things I've already done. And even if I could do new things, like climbing Mount Everest, okay maybe that's too much, let's say climbing the Abetone mountain, what would I need these new things for, which are not new? After all, five minutes are enough to understand how life works, to smell the scent of the air, the gusts of wind, the weight of our steps, everything else is redundant.

So, I'd rather just stay here, it's not like I want to kill myself, I do like living, but I want to stop *doing*, I just want to *think*, to *remember*. I have a collection of memories, they are all beautiful memories, at least some, others a bit less, though bad memories, you know, are beautiful too. Memories have this particular property, that allows you to change perspective. It is worth going through your memories carefully, rather than waiting for old age to do it. I want to do it now, I want to take advantage of the fact that they are re-emerging in a random order, like April 2nd, 1992 next to September 5th, 2004, my first bicycle next to my Peugeot 205—a gift from my father before he left for Argentina—, Caterina Magri alongside all the girls I met at university.

I read in the newspaper

I read in the newspaper that my mother brought me this morning [you have to stay updated on events, she told me], of an American guy who came up with this idea of owning a maximum of one hundred objects. Interesting. One hundred objects are not that many in today's world, out there. If one starts to count clothes and then furniture, ornaments, cutlery, dishes and so on, there you have it, your one hundred objects. This American guy must have thrown a lot of stuff away.

Of course, here in the hospital world, it's easier to live with few things. Two pajamas (four objects, counting the top and the bottom), three shirts and three underpants (that makes six more objects), three pairs of socks (six more objects here, too), a pen and a notebook (add two), the computer that Karin brought me (which I could do without), two reference books (*Oblomov, A Man Asleep*). Total: twenty-one objects.

I forgot toothpaste, a toothbrush and hospital slippers. That makes twenty-four. Obviously, this is doable because I am in a hospital. I will never get out (of the hospital), but if I do, I would like to live in a furnished rental house. This avoids owning dishes, cutlery and a sofa. There are several advantages, that is, when it comes to moving. When you move, you just leave everything there, except your clothes and a few personal items.

Twenty-four objects won't be enough, it's cold out there, I can tell when I look out the window in the morning, there's plenty of frost on the lawn. Starting from a basis of the twenty-four objects, one can add:

two pairs of pants (summer and winter)

two pairs of shoes (summer and winter)

a sweatshirt

a sweater

a heavy jacket

a light jacket

(total, eight more items to add)

That makes thirty-two already.

What else does one need? I can't think of anything else. Maybe it's because I have been hiding here for three months, I can't really think of anything else. A windbreaker if it rains, a Swiss army knife . . . that makes thirty-four. Nothing else comes to mind. Two towels, that's thirty-six. A large backpack and a small backpack, that's thirty-eight.

That's it. It reminds me of when I make a list of what I need to take on a trip. A few months before the accident, I went on a trip through the Baltic countries, then Russia, and then Greece. Three months, through various climates and seasons. I only had eight kilos of stuff in my backpack. More or less the thirty-eight objects I was talking about.

Of course, one thing is to travel, and another thing is to be sedentary. Objects pile up every day. I am sure I forgot something that I couldn't do without if I lived out there. Already in my house I have way more than thirty-eight objects that belong to me. For example, books and old T-shirts and other objects, memories of distant journeys. If I count the books, that's it, there go your one hundred objects. As a solution, one could donate them to the library and go and read them every now and then. The same goes for old shirts and other memories, I mean, one could come up with some kind of memory-storage of stuff that is not really needed but that consists of memories. Everyone is given a cubic meter of memories or even a bit less, and then one puts them all in the memory-storage. Whenever you feel like it, you can go and see your own memories, or even those of others, which is kind of like going to see someone, instead you go to see his or her memories, which is almost the same thing, or perhaps even better.

It's just a big bluff!

It's just a big bluff! The American minimalist! Obviously, he has a blog, I found it right away, and there it is, his list of one hundred objects, that is, ninety-six objects, because he wanted to leave himself a little bit of slack, the American minimalist. But there is also a premise! And the premise says that everyday objects (shared with his wife or children) do not count. And he doesn't even tell us what they are! He may own three shared flat-screen televisions and we wouldn't even know it. He could have a shared satellite stereo, a shared sailboat, along with all the buoys and sails, and he wouldn't tell us, since that wouldn't count anyways.

And then the books, when I think that I'm feeling guilty about them, I would give them to the library. What does he do instead? He doesn't count them! Books don't matter! (Except for the Bible, that counts, and he has two). What about underpants? Of course, he doesn't count them one by one. He may have two hundred pairs of underpants, he counts them as one single mega-underpant.

So much for the minimalist! At any rate, I too, thanks to my mother, have a new object now. She came by before dinner, she was in a hurry because she had another condominium meeting.

She left me a new mobile phone with a new number and every-thing. She told me she would call me after dinner and she did. She told me about her condominium meeting, and all of the condominium injustices. Can you believe that all the expenses, even the water bills, are divided equally per apartment, even if I live on my own, said my mother, while there are five people in the Curatolo family, who knows how much water they use? But I, now that your father is gone, am alone, how much water do you think I'm going to use? And then there's the elevator, did I tell you about that? We split the elevator bills too, but I'm on the first floor, what do you want me to use the elevator for? But let's just forget about all these ridiculous condominium affairs, they're so ridiculous, they really get on my nerves when I think about them . . . Anyways, what about you, how are you? Well . . . I told her, I'm here . . . And Simone, did you call him? Please call him, Simone, now that you have a mobile phone, you know that he has to go to Munich every week, it's because his Milan branch has closed, I told you about that, didn't I? Now he has to go to Munich, at least call him every now and then, and also Uncle Beppe, you should call him too, that way you can ask him about the operation . . . They sent him home, he is stuck there, poor thing, he went through two operations, two operations to-gether, six hours under the knife, call him, with all he had to go through, that procedure, it could have finished him off. Please just call him, I'm sure he will appreciate it, you have the num-ber, right? If not, I can give it to you, I'll send it to you with an sms, okay? I have the number, I told her. You got it? If not, I'll send it to you. I have it, I have it. Okay, you have it, but if you don't, I can send it to you, I will send you a text message, so if you don't find the number, you will have it in my message . . .

Okay then, come on, try to get better, don't you worry, you'll see that you'll get better soon . . . What else did I want to tell you . . . right, Aunt Lidia called me, your cousin Silvana is getting married, did you know that she was getting married, or did you forget about it? . . . Well, she's getting married next week, we're all going to be there, at least give her a call, and get in touch with Aunt Lidia, okay? Do you have Aunt Lidia's number? . . . If not, I can send it to you, I'll send it to you together with Uncle Beppe's number . . . Okay then, so don't worry, and then call Simone, you can find him on Sunday, you know that every week he has to go to Munich . . . and Uncle Beppe too . . . call him too. Okay Mom, I told her, I'll call them. Fine then, I'll send you all the numbers with an sms, so that you call them all, c'mon, you'll be alright, don't you worry.

Tonight, for dinner

Tonight, for dinner, they brought me:

1) Alphabet soup. It was full of A's, but there were also some C's, and Z's, or maybe they were N's? A few pieces of spinach were floating on the surface of the soup, like so many icebergs, only that they were not cold.

2) A piece of chicken served with a mound of spinach. The same spinach that had accidentally fallen into the soup? I ate all the chicken, interspersing it with bites of the spinach mound, trying to pick up the lateral spinach first, so that the mound could stand up as long as possible. Eventually it fell to the side, and I finished it.

3) Fruit arranged like some kind of fruit salad. There were also small green pieces, but they were not spinach.

I don't know if they will bring me food indefinitely, which would be convenient because my intentions are to stay here forever. I asked a nurse, she replied threateningly that I have almost recovered.

You will walk again

You will walk again, Gustavo, or Guglielmo, a name that begins with G, which I can never remember, the hospital physiotherapist, told me this morning. But he didn't sound very convincing. Maybe not run, he added, but walk, that's for sure. As he said these things, the sun peeked through the gaps between the hospital buildings, and seemed to agree with him.

I don't know, I told him, for now I'm struggling, especially with my left leg. You have three bones in that leg, Giacomo told me, and they were all broken. Of course, you're struggling. To start with, you will walk on crutches, in a couple of weeks you will leave the hospital and then you will come here to do physiotherapy in day hospital.

Can't I stay here a little longer, instead of coming to day hospital, I would already be here . . . The beds are expensive, he told me, and you are almost fine now, Gianfranco cut short. Or Girolamo. I just can't remember his name. I don't seem to be able to remember certain names. If I don't remember them the first time, then I don't remember them ever. It must be because of how badly I hit my head on the ground, a head injury with a third-degree retrograde mnemonic deficit, as was written on the report. It seems that certain names elude me, I simply cannot retain them.

Yet I remember the names of all the children in my first-grade class, but I can't remember the name of the physiotherapist. I'm sure it starts with G, but a soft G like Gerolamo, or a hard one like Guglielmo? I am already struggling on the type of G. Instead, my first-grade classmates, I remember them all, there was Fabio Tilli who went skiing in Cervinia every Sunday and returned tanned on Monday, there was Marco Marasco who, on his way back home from school, walked with me and then we said to each other, See you tomorrow, unfortunately! There was Roberto Stasi who one day got up holding his bottom with one hand and asked the teacher, Can I go poop? And then of course there was Caterina Magri, who was supposed to faint but never did.

In addition to Gustavo the physiotherapist

In addition to Gustavo the physiotherapist, Broglia the doctor, Danovaro the Marshal and Lorenzo the kid, there is a male nurse, Piero, and three female nurses, Laura, Rita and Katia, who come to visit us. Piero is a big guy but he doesn't move much, as if all those muscles are inhibiting him instead of giving him strength. Laura, on the other hand, is skinny to the bone, but very energetic. If there is anything that needs to be moved, she deals with it, rather than Piero, who prefers to stand in the corner and check. What it is that he checks, I wouldn't know, perhaps that Dr. Braglia does not come by and find out that he is not working. Laura never speaks, she only points at things with her hands. If she wants you to pass the tray, she points to the tray and then withdraws her hand as if to indicate the direction that the tray must take, that is, from me to her. Rita is the unpleasant one, I mean she is the one who keeps threatening me by saying that I have finally recovered, she says every day that I have re-covered now, what am I still doing here? And when she brings me food she tells me, Here is the pasta soup for our *imaginary patient*, or, Here is a slice of chicken for our *sleeping beauty*. She always makes a lot of allusions when she talks about me. Then there is Katia the sweet one. Katia seems to be the only one who cares about me, she asks me, How's it going today, a good question, and I tell her, It's going, it's going . . . She listens and says, That's better, and then she makes my bed and I shiver while I look at her making my bed, all this attention has always made me shiver, I'm not sure why. Then she helps me to go back to bed gently and consequently there is more shivering that comes with all this attention.

It doesn't matter that she gets paid, that this is her job. My shivers don't know this or don't care, they come to me no matter what. The other night I dreamt of her, Katia. There was this huge bed that she had made for me and then she said to me, Come on, get ready and I didn't understand what there was to get ready for. Come on, get ready, and then she went to bed first and gave me her hand. It was a beautiful dream full of shiver-producing care.

And then, all the nurses wear those white clogs, Dr. Scholl's clogs, but only Katia has ankles that are worthwhile, that is, the ankles Dr. Scholl had in mind when he invented Dr. Scholl's clogs. Those ankles that one can see coming out of Dr. Scholl's clogs make me shiver, just thinking that they are the same ankles that Katia wears when she is at home and makes the beds at home with the same attention she has for mine.

Her hands, she has some hands, Katia, that are also definitely worth looking at. Her hands are not too well-groomed, so one can see they are working hands but are still beautiful, elongated and firm, when they grab the sheets and the blankets and rearrange them. I try to guess where they are hiding between the folds to get some shivers while she is busy with all this attention for me. Actually, she makes all the beds, even the Marshal's and Lorenzo's, but I had the impression that she was paying more attention to mine. So yesterday I measured it, I counted the time it took her to make my bed then the Marshal's and Lorenzo's and I won by a lot, that is, four minutes and twenty seconds for my bed against barely two minutes for the Marshal's and Lorenzo's. It could be argued that my bed is more unmade, and that is why it takes her longer, but that isn't true because she rearranges everything from scratch, it doesn't matter how unmade a bed is, I am the winner as far as attention goes. When she is done making the beds, and is about to leave, she always asks, Is everything okay? Do you need anything? And she says it to me not to the others, she must know that it makes me shiver, maybe it's part of my therapy? I usually answer, Everything is okay, but I shiver at the thought of what would happen if everything was not okay, what would she do with her elongated hands and her ankles peeking out from Dr. Scholl's clogs, she would immediately do something to make me shiver even more.

Do you know what keywords are?

Do you know what keywords are? my niece Luisa asks me. My mother came this morning and brought Luisa with her and left her here with me while she went outside to call the administrator on the phone. What keywords? I ask her. We learned them at school, Uncle Lapo, Luisa tells me, for every story, even for books, there are keywords. For a book, five keywords. And how does it work? I ask her. Tell me a book, so that I can show you how it works, she says. I tell her Little Red Riding Hood. Easy, she says, *riding hood, snack, grandmother, wolf, hunter.* Good, I tell her, and what about Snow White? Even easier, she says, *dwarves, stepmother, mirror, apple, prince.* Nice! I tell her.

And for any sentences, two keywords are enough, two keywords say it all, you'll see, she tells me. Tell me a sentence, so that I can show you how it works, Uncle Lapo. Okay, here it is, today Dr. Braglia came to visit us, then you came with your grandmother. And she goes *doctor, grandmother.* So I tell her, yesterday Rome won one to zero, and she goes *Rome, won.*

What if I tell you something more complicated? I ask her, like some songs? Try it, uncle Lapo, she replies. At the Oriental fair my father bought a mouse, I tell her. And she goes, *fair, mouse.* And if I tell you Rome, don't be silly tonight? *Rome, silly,* she says.

And what about proverbs? I ask her. Even easier, she says, there is really no need to say the whole proverb, two keywords are enough. When the cat's away, the mice will play? I ask her. *Cat, mice,* she says. See?

Meanwhile, my mother comes back. Guess what the administrator wants to do now? He wants to change the heating system! *Administrator, heating,* says Luisa. He wants to do it now, says my mother, we're in April, it's still chilly, but he can't wait for summer, of course not, he wants to have it done right away so the whole house will be cold! *April, cold,* says Luisa. What are you saying, Luisa? Nothing, Mom, Luisa is practicing an exercise for her school, I tell my mother, while I wink at Luisa.

Okay, we have to go now. I have to prepare dinner for Simone, tonight he's coming back from Munich, you knew that, right? Did you call him? (*Simone, Munich*). Sure, Mom, I will call him. Please call him, I gave you a cell phone for a reason, why don't you call Simone, he is your brother (*Simone, telephone*). Yes, Mom, I told you, I will call him. And also, Uncle Beppe, call him too, now that you have your own cell phone (*telephone, Uncle Beppe*).

If his brain hasn't melted yet

If his brain hasn't melted yet, I mean Lorenzo's brain, the kid on the bed to my right, I bet it's going to happen one day or another. He just lies down there tinkering on his video games, always there, in the same position, also because he has one leg in traction and therefore cannot move. On my left, the Marshal snores away, interrupted only by some loud farts, or by his trying to chat me up with his ideas about the captain of the Rome team, sometimes he watches the television that they let him keep in our room.

At least, on my left, the landscape changes every now and again. On my right, however, it is always the same. Every now and then Lorenzo's parents stop by and bring him a new toy. He has so many of those little toys that if he puts them one on top of the other on his bedside table, it looks like the Tower of Pisa. He opens his new game, pulls out some kind of chip and puts it in his Nintendo device, DS as he calls it. He starts playing while his parents talk to him, after a while his mother beckons him to stop and he says, Wait, I'm not done with my game yet! Then his parents leave and he keeps tinkering with his video games.

Lorenzo never talks to us, I mean with me and the Marshal. The Marshal occasionally tries to get him involved in soccer matches, but he doesn't respond. At which point we ask a nurse to set up the TV between our two beds, me and the Marshal, and we watch a soccer game with no audio.

Today while they took the Marshal down

Today while they took the Marshal down to do his physiotherapy, I asked Lorenzo to show me how his little game works. He was taking a break, meaning that he was changing the chip in his game, and I told him, Hey Lorenzo, how does this game work? What do you mean? he answered me. Can you show it to me, or is it too difficult? What do you mean? What? What do you mean?

I mean, if I wanted to . . . since after all we are both stuck here for quite some time, if you could explain to me how it works . . . Sure, but there are lots of games, he said. Well, yeah, maybe you can show me an easy one, for starter, right? This one? he asked me. Sure, whichever one, I told him. Okay then, just a second . . . so, here's Mario, it's actually a bit difficult, because . . . you have to . . . so, with this you can move, with the "A" you can jump, with the darts you can move, okay, and these are the basic commands. You have to try to get to the next level. Then there are these things, the yellow cubes, with question marks, when you're under them, you have to jump and hit them and usually you get stronger. The first time you do it you get some kind of mushroom, and then you get bigger. The second time, on the other hand, you get this kind of flower and you become fire. And when you are, say, fire, you can shoot fire balls, and eliminate the opponent. And what is the ultimate goal of the game, in the end? I asked him. The ultimate goal is to get to the end of the castle. That is, there are different worlds, for example, here, you see, this is world six. World six is characterized by rocks, world three by sea, world five by ice, and you always have to get to the end of the last castle, which would be world eight. I can try, I said. Yes, of course, but . . . just a sec, one more thing, there's also enemies, right? That's all the things that move, those are your enemies, and you have to jump on them. If instead you bump into them this other way, you see, here, then you get hurt.

Then he reached out to me from his bed, to show me his DS, you see, this is the button to go to the right, this one to the left, then up, down, this other one to jump, and this one to shoot. If you want, I have two of them, I can lend you one. Are you sure? I asked him. Of course, of course, I can only use one at a time, so just start at level one, remember that you have to take the flowers to become fire or the yellow cubes to become bigger, here, take it.

So I find myself walking around world one, a world where Mario with his blue and red jumpsuit goes around shooting and jumping across ditches, to take flowers or yellow cubes, all with a background that could be Dubai, a somewhat futuristic and Arabic city at the same time. Lorenzo occasionally peeks out of his bed to see how well I'm managing. It seems to me that I am doing badly, for now, they have already killed me twice, or I have fallen into a ravine, but I don't care, I can start from scratch if I have to, I don't see the problem, I have a lot of time to get there, I mean to the castle. I've already died several times today.

It turns out that there are many other things to do. You have to break these boxes full of money, you have to watch out for mushrooms because they can kill you, and for the holes because otherwise you fall into them, and every now and then a chimney shows up, which you can go into and a new world opens up for you.

This morning I got to play

This morning I got to play with my DS (which is not mine, of course, it's Lorenzo's DS). I avoided the ravines, I jumped one ditch after another as if it was nothing, I was doing quite well, and while I was doing quite well, I heard some kind of flutter, must be some special sound effects I said to myself as I entered a forest world with Mario hopping away. Instead, those were not special sound effects.

It was a little bird, a sparrow-like passerine that probably had come in the window when Rita opened it while saying, How can you stay in here with this stench? and the Marshal replied with a major fart. Then Rita closed the window and left, the Marshal went back to sleep, and Lorenzo and I kept playing with our DS's (mine was actually the one he lent me, he has two, I've got none, that's how it works here).

We were playing with our DS's, the Marshal was sleeping and the passerine was fluttering between the ceiling and the window. We didn't say anything. We hadn't seen a passerine in months. Actually none of us were really looking at it, not the Marshal since he was asleep, not Lorenzo nor I because we were busy playing with our DS's (which were Lorenzo's, both of them, he had only lent me one), we were so busy playing that, at most, we could barely hear the flutter of the passerine.

It had been months since we had last heard anything flutter, so we kind of enjoyed it. But that's when Rita comes back and finds out and starts screaming, Oh my God! There's a beast in here! Pierooo!

She starts screaming Pierooo! but Laura shows up. It always worked that way, whatever Piero was supposed to do, Laura did, if you called Piero, you'd always get Laura. Here's Laura, What is it? she asks. There's a beast! A beast! Rita screams while getting a broom. She screams and slams her broom against the poor passerine, which is luckily quite elusive, and can avoid those randomly-directed broom shots without any problems. Rita keeps screaming and when the passerine decides that it is time to move out of the way, away from the window and Rita's frantic blows, and flies over our beds, Rita starts to jump between one bed and the other as if she was possessed. So much so that the Marshal finally wakes up, Hey?! What's going on? What the hell!? At which Rita tries to explain, There's a beast, can't you see? Here it is, the bloody beast, I'll take care of it! Holy shit, says the Marshal, is she out of her mind or what?

Finally, the others, Piero and Katia, arrive as well. Piero stands in a corner and watches the scene. This time Laura does not know what to do, luckily there's Katia, Katia the sweet. Without saying anything, she goes near the window, opens it, pulls back the curtains, and so the passerine zigzags between Rita's blows, and gets out of there without further ado.

Done. Then Katia leaves, silently just like she arrived, without taking any glory, as real heroes do. Piero chuckles, while Laura and Rita leave full of embarrassment. This whole time Lorenzo hasn't stopped playing his game for a second. I, on the other hand, have stopped my game. I had almost reached the sixth world when Rita came in and started screaming and jumping around, so now I have to start over. The Marshal finds nothing else to say but, Gee, what a madhouse! and goes back to snoring.

I'm left here on my bed, without knowing exactly what to do. I'm holding the DS in my hand, but now I'm somewhere else in my head. It's as if I can still hear the flutter of the passerine, but no, it's the Marshal who is snoring. The nurses are all gone. Lorenzo remained impassive, he didn't give a damn about the passerine. I look at him in admiration. I want to peek, to check what level he's at, but I'm afraid to find out that he's already in the tenth or twentieth world. I don't even know if they exist, my best score was when I reached the seventh world, last night.

The professional DS player distinguishes himself from the beginner especially in this kind of situation, when for example a passerine shows up. The professional player does not get distracted, he keeps jumping from one world to the other undeterred. I, on the other hand, lost all concentration because of the passerine. Now it's useless to even try to start playing again, no way, I just can't.

But what was the passerine thinking, flying into a hospital room? They say that animals have a personality just like us, they can be shy or bold, there is a gradient from the shyest, to the intermediate, to the very bold. For example, bold birds, if you put them in a new environment, like a room with trees they've never seen before, they immediately begin to explore, while the shy ones remain still. This passerine must have been one of the bold ones, as soon as he spotted a hole in the half-open window of our room, he slipped into it. Even simpler animals, lower vertebrates such as fish, and even invertebrates, it turns out that they too, have a personality. We had already seen it in our laboratory, the shy fish took a long time to come out of their shelter. Everything revolves around being shy or bold.

In reality, there is no winning strategy. Simply, bold individuals are those who have a higher metabolism, grow faster and need to eat more. That's why they are bold, they look for any opportunity. But this does not mean that they have an advantage in life compared to the shy ones, because being bold also means taking more risks. So being shy or bold are just two alternative strategies, what works best changes from one situation to another. In the case of the passerine, if it had got a broom in the face from Rita, that would have been the end of it.

The same goes for humans. Of course, our personalities are very complex, there are the creative ones, the nice ones, the superficial one, the ones who get easily irritated. But perhaps it mainly boils down to being shy or bold. There seems to be a special gene that regulates our sense of courage. Whoever has the courage trait is bolder, it seems. Not that things work better for the bold. From an evolutionary point of view, being bold works well especially when the environment changes constantly. But if things stay the way they are, being shy is just fine.

Here in the hospital, the environment and the situations don't change much. There is no point in being bold here, you just have to stay in bed waiting, collecting memories, playing with them (even if now I have a hard time doing that). I adapt.

When I was out, I remember quite well, I often went on long random trips on my own. I hitchhiked, I didn't even know exactly where I was going, I went along with the people who gave me a ride. What mattered to me was to go somewhere. What mattered was to get away from my everyday life. Now I have found a much simpler, unexpected solution. Staying here is even easier. So I put the DS on the bedside table. Lorenzo continues his ascent to worlds higher and higher. The Marshal turns over in his bed. Outside there are passerines that peek inside timidly.

When I met you

When I met you, you were not like this, you had a lot of friends, you were always going someplace, Karin told me today. You did a lot of things, you played the guitar, you wrote poetry, you read books. I still read books, I told her, look here, and I pointed to *Oblomov* and *A Man Asleep*. Beautiful books, she said, just suitable for you! *A Man Asleep*! And the other one, what's the other one about? I bet it's not an action book, huh? Not really, I told her. See? See? she told me.

And then what is that thing you have on the bedside table? she asked me, Shhh, I whispered, so that Lorenzo couldn't hear me, it's the DS Lorenzo lent me. What did you borrow? Are you going back to being a kid? Come on, I told her, don't make a big deal, otherwise Lorenzo could hear us and get offended. Gosh, you really are a big baby then, she continued, and I made the gesture with my hand to be quiet, I didn't want to offend Lorenzo, otherwise maybe he'll want his DS back.

Now I'm going to ask you a question, she said, I'm curious to hear what you answer; why did you marry me? I don't know,

I told her, we decided that way, it was also easier to get your residence permit. At this point she insisted, I knew it! A marriage of convenience! No, c'mon, I told her, we were together, we decided we might as well get married so that everything would be easier since we were together anyways. What do you mean, WE WERE? Yes, we were, we are. WE WERE or WE ARE? But it's the same thing, isn't it the same thing? It is NOT the same, she said. It is not the same thing, I repeated. Is it not the same thing? she asked.

How am I supposed to know, I mean, you ask yourself the questions and then you answer them, I told her. Sure, the questions, she said, it's not a matter of questions, it's that you're lying on your ass here while I'm out there working. Now you're here too, I told her. Don't play word games, you know I don't like them . . . anyways when are you going to get out of here? The physiotherapist said I would be ready in a couple of weeks . . . Well then, are you getting out in two weeks? I didn't say that, I said I would be ready. And isn't it the same thing? It's not the same thing, the physiotherapist said I'd be ready, but I don't know. What don't you know? I don't know anything anymore, I'm confused, I mix things up, same with names, memories, dreams. What do you mean, where does that come from? she asked.

From nowhere, I told her, it doesn't come from anywhere. And what does *coming from* mean, anyways, I thought we're talking about *getting out*, not *coming from*. Lapo, you're so full of shit, she said, Okay I am full of shit. So stop it, she said. Okay, I'll stop it. At this point she turned and left, Karin. And I went back to reading *A Man Asleep* and fell asleep.

There is that song

There is that song called "The Sound of Silence." Sounds like a pretty good idea to me. But then Simon & Garfunkel made it into a real song, and that was the end of the silence. John Cage did better, he composed a piece of four minutes and thirty-three seconds of silence. You can play it with any instrument, but it is especially good with string instruments. The absence of string instruments is very pleasant when there is silence. Here in the hospital there is a lot of silence. It's not always the same silence. There is the silence after my mother has left, which is different from the silence after Malvezzi, Dr. Braglia or even Katia have left. When Karin leaves, then, there is a nice reassuring silence, which is why I often fall asleep when she leaves.

Months ago, I mean when I was out, that is, out there with the others, with Malvezzi, Karin and all the others, there was always this never-ending concert. I played too, everybody played, I don't even remember if there was a pause between one song and the other. I guess there wasn't one. Now they all take turns coming here and telling me, Play Lapo, play! But what am I supposed to play? People like to give advice. This thing is very strange. In my opinion, they are all jealous that I have found this pretty smart solution of the hospital, and they do not want me to get away with it. They have realized that I have put away all the chess pieces and decided not to play anymore. Or, to go back to the musical metaphor, I have put the violin back in its case.

Anyways, while I was at it, I went back to sleep with Karin's silence after she was gone. When I woke up, it was very hot. From the clock in the room, I saw it was five in the morning, the Marshal and Lorenzo were still sleeping. They must have cranked up the heating, I thought. The ceiling was spinning around. I was in a cold sweat.

It occurred to me that I might have a fever. A fever in these cases can help lengthen the stay. It wouldn't be a bad thing if I had a lengthening fever. Katia could certainly bring out special treatments that she reserves only for special fever-patients. There is a special switch for these cases, there is a switch above the bed, one presses the switch and the nurse comes to see what is going on.

The problem is that in these cases any nurse, Piero, Laura, Rita or Katia, could show up. One would need to know who is working the night shift. I tried to, I came up with a file on the computer with the sequence of those who did the previous night shifts, which I only figured out when one of us three needed help. That is, almost every night, because the Marshal always has some problem at night. The other day he started to quiver after the Roma game, it looked like an epileptic attack, they had to give him a shot.

At the beginning, the sequence started out as Laura, Rita, Piero, Katia, but then whenever you are expecting Laura to show up again after Katia, there comes Piero instead. That doctor Broglia is one step ahead of the devil, he must have invented a very complicated algorithm for establishing the night shifts. Rather than ringing the bell so that Rita shows up just to tell me—here is our imaginary patient!—I'm staying here sweating like mad, hoping that Katia will be the first one to find out.

Instead, neither Katia nor Rita found out about my fever, but Piero. He told me, Hey, you feel hot! and called a doctor who, however, was not Dr. Broglia but a replacement. Eventually it turned out that I had got a urinary infection. They gave me antibiotics. I have a high fever, so I am a little out of it when my mother calls me.

Was it you who called me a few minutes ago? she asks me. No, Mom, I didn't call you. So who could it have been? This thing makes me anxious, people call me and then they don't call back. Yep, I tell her. And how are you doing today, Lapo? she asks me. I have a bit of a fever, I tell her. How much of a fever? she asks me. Fever fever I tell her. But what kind of a fever? About a hundred and two, I tell her. But how did you get a fever? she asks me. I don't know, I just got it like that, at night. But how, at night? she keeps asking. How could it be, at night? It was night, I tell her, it was dark outside so it was at night. She insists, But . . . and the doctors, what are the doctors saying? Were there any doctors around? Yes, the doctors were there, I tell her, I have a urinary infection. What do you mean, a urinary infection? Like a urinary infection, I tell her. And so? she asks me. So nothing, they gave me antibiotics. And now what are you going to do? Do what? There's nothing to do, only antibiotics to take. I'll be there soon, she says, but first I have a condominium meeting because the administrator has decided to have the facade painted, just what I need! The facade! But do you know what that means? I tell you what it means, Lapo, it means that they will put the scaffolding up, so if thieves want to sneak into my house, all they have to do is to get on the scaffolding, that's how I get thieves in my house, can you believe it? Every time he comes up with some wonderful new idea, this administrator. He doesn't care, the thieves will visit my house, not his!

Anyways, have you called Uncle Beppe? No, Mom, I haven't called him. Please call him, what are you waiting for, and call

Aunt Lidia and Simone too, now you have your cell phone, why don't you use it? Now I have to go to the meeting, I can't believe the things I have to do if I don't want thieves in my house, a condo meeting, just what I need. I hate these meetings, but I have to go, then I'll come see you. Okay, goodbye then, I tell her, I'm going to sleep now. Goodbye then, she says, but please call your Uncle Beppe, he just got out of the hospital today, of all days, it's terrible timing, have you looked at the weather outside? There's a hell of a wind out there, you should see the mess on the streets! It's howling like OOOOhhhhhh . . . I've never seen a wind like this, it's hard to believe one's eyes, you're better off staying where you are, this wind can blow you off the ground, and I have to go to the condo meeting . . . And you know what else the administrator said? That now we have to start recycling! Just what I need! He sent us twenty pages of instructions, the administrator, can you believe it, twenty pages! Is he out of his mind? Twenty pages, and then for what? To explain that there will be colors, but what colors? It turns out that it'll be green for regular garbage, yellow for compost, red for plastic, and that's not even it! There'll be lots of bins, can you imagine how beautiful the garden will look with these bins? There won't be any more space to walk, with all these bins, just bins, bins everywhere.

And then listen to this, in the residual urban waste, so that's what is called now, in the residual urban waste there are audio and video tapes, CDs, plates, buckets, toys, ballpoint pens, basins . . . I mean, what do they all want from me? I can find a couple of broken ballpoint pens, but where do I find the video tapes? And the CDs? I have never used them, the CDs, what am I supposed to do now?

But let's not talk about it anymore, this recycling business really drives me up the wall. What about you, why don't you call Uncle Beppe, he would be happy to hear from you. Yes, I tell her, Okay, I will call him, now I am going to sleep a little bit, I'm quite tired, so goodbye . . . Okay she says, Bye then, goodbye but please call Uncle Beppe, Simone called him, you know, he even called him from Munich, you should call him too, and while you're at it, call Simone as well . . .

No way, there was no way out. So I put my cell phone on the table and let myself lie back on my bed. I hear the distant hum of my mother's voice insisting, but I'm too weak to do anything other than sleep.

I was sound asleep

I was sound asleep because of the medicines they gave me to treat my urinary infection. I had a pretty rough night, judging by the knotted blankets. I must have had some nightmares, but I don't remember much. All I can remember is a beautiful dream in which I was a coral reef fish, a bit like Nemo, which I had seen with my niece Luisa.

But I was not a clown fish, I was just a regular fish, a small goby, queuing at a cleaning station. These cleaning stations really exist in the sea, there are cleaner fish that clean parasites from other fish as well as other things that are left between their teeth, in their gills, and on their skin.

I was there in the queue. It was me but I was also a fish. And all the other fish I could see were fish but also people I know. My mother was a big grouper, they were already cleaning her while I was in the queue. Karin, she was there too, was a stingray, resting on the sand next to me. I wanted to ask her if she too was waiting to get cleaned, but I didn't know how.

Of course, Malvezzi was there too, he was a fake cleaner fish, one of those fish that look like real cleaner fish, but that instead of cleaning, they eat bits of the customers' fins. It was to be expected of someone like Malvezzi. It was already surprising that he himself was acting like the false cleaning fish and did not have someone else stealing the food for him. I was waiting for my turn, and I tried not to look at Malvezzi who meanwhile was biting some young fish that couldn't tell the difference between real and fake cleaner fish.

My turn was late in coming. My mother the grouper had started talking with the cleaner fish and it was never ending. I had to have my gills cleaned as soon as possible. They were full of junk, and it was hard for me to breathe. I need my gills, I thought, I started to ventilate them as much as I could, but it was not enough, they were too clogged. The stingray looked at me sideways as if my hyperventilation was getting on her nerves. I was stuck between a high-maintenance client such as the grouper and a stingray full of herself. In the end, I was the one who suffered, I had a hard time breathing and couldn't wait any longer for my turn.

I was so desperate that I was almost about to entrust myself to Malvezzi, the fake cleaner fish. I would have even let him chew on my fins as long as he cleaned my gills a little. But then, almost magically, it was my turn. The grouper and all the other fish in the line had finished and left.

I swam a little bit forward to put myself in the center of the cleaning station. I opened the opercula that covered my gills and a nice cleaner fish showed up and started cleaning my gills gently. Needless to say, it was Katia, I could tell from the way she cleaned me with her magic touch. Katia cleaned my gills, and I was ecstatic. Not to mention that I was no longer out of breath, my gills had started to function again. In the distance, I could see the stingray who was giving me the evil eye. To hell with the stingray, I thought, I was having a great time, getting all my ins and outs cleaned by Katia the cleaner fish.

When I wake up

When I wake up, I see Karin, I mean the real one, standing right there in front of me, and looking at me. I am awake but pretend to be asleep and for a few minutes it works. It's like going back in time, when Karin was not a stingray but that woman who held my hand and I didn't know who she was. Then she says, Lapo, and I answer huh, and the spell is gone. Do you still have a fever? Your mother called me and told me you have a fever. Maybe, I tell her, a fever is a good thing, it means that there is someone in there who is busy. At which she goes, right, at least there's someone working, while you sleep all day.

I do not say anything. She adds, You have two gears, Lapo, you've always had two gears, that's right, two gears . . . Huh, and what gears would they be? I ask her. Well, I think that's pretty obvious, you're either in fourth or first, or rather, in idle. Either you're all busy traveling, working, like in full swing, or you're lying there doing nothing. This thing drives me crazy, I can't stand it, you just have no middle ground, not at all.

And now would I be in idle? I ask her. Well, yeah, that's pretty clear to me, she says, more idle than that, I would say that's perfectly spot on. Lapo, don't you remember when we were in Greece? Sure, I tell her, I remember. You, says Karin, never stopped, while I wanted to rest, every now and then. We were on vacation, for me vacation equals rest, but not for you, as soon as we arrived on an island you started to explore all the more distant ravines, you left on foot in the morning and came back in the evening, while I stayed back to read to or go for a swim. And then no island was good enough for you, there were always too many tourists even if in reality there were only four cats at most. It was late September, but for you even a couple of tourists were always too many. In the end, we landed on some kind of a rock where there were only a couple of goats, and you were finally happy. I, on the other hand, want to see people, Lapo, not all the time, but often, and then I also want to rest every now and then, and take walks but not go crazy like you do. Or rather, like *you did,* now it seems to me that you're not walking that much.

What do you want me to say? I tell her, which wasn't the best thing to say, as I realized immediately, in fact she said, I don't want you to tell me anything, Lapo, you have become an amoeba, you can only say *Sure,* or *what you want me to tell you,* but c'mon, there is a whole world out there and instead you are here, you have finally recovered even if you seem quite happy that this providential fever has come to you. I really don't understand you, what is it that bothers you? What are you trying to avoid? You don't want to work anymore?

I don't know what to say, so I tell her Malvezzi. Malvezzi, what does Malvezzi have to do with it? I don't want to be like Malvezzi, I tell her. She looks at me and goes, But nobody is forcing you to become like Malvezzi. Although he does seem like a nice guy. And anyways, what is that about? You are you and

Malvezzi is Malvezzi. I don't see the problem. It's not by being locked up here that you can solve your problems. Being locked up here, you miss out on a lot of things, tons of things! Think about it, Lapo, think about your previous life, and about what you're doing now, or rather, what you're not doing now. Are you sure it's okay with you? I'll think about it, I tell her to reassure her. Well, that's better than nothing, better than nothing, she says, and in saying so, she says goodbye and leaves.

One thing I've seen people do in America

One thing I've seen people do in America when they have to make a decision is a nice list with all the pros and cons. In reality, people usually already know what they want to do, and the list is just an excuse to justify what they will come up with. I had seen Karin do it too, she had studied in America. I could make a list, a list in which I write down what I was doing before and what I am doing now, just to make a comparison. I grab the computer and start writing.

Main activity
Before: Working as a biologist at the Ecosystem Center.
Now: Resting on this bed, collecting memories, reading *Oblomov* and *A Man Asleep*, over and over.

Leisure
Before: Traveling, cycling, going to the movies with Karin.
Now: Resting on this bed, collecting memories, reading . . .

Oh, I get it! I realize that a fundamental difference is that in my current situation there is no dividing line between duty and pleasure. Not that everything has to be duty or pleasure, it's just that what I do has no such connotation. I have no duty, no pleasure. There is a cycle out there, come to think of it, there is a cycle in which I was involved as well as everyone else, a cycle that makes you carry out your duty, and then do something you like. Even when we were kids, our parents told us, first you do your homework and then you can go out to play. It's this cycle that wrecks the whole world, why must there be a cycle, why must duty be separated from pleasure? It's a mistake, it's a big mistake, and I had to come here, to this hospital, to find out, because here it's clear that there is no difference between duty and pleasure.

This is why I don't want to go out there and be put back at the crossroads between doing things out of duty or pleasure. Even the weekend, here, weekends do not exist, though one can tell from the flow of people if it's Saturday or Sunday. But the primitives had no weekend, and that was the right thing to do. When I think about what is right, I always think of the primitives, there's no doubt they were right, I always say to myself. No doubt, because they were still animals, they had not yet proclaimed themselves humans, above nature.

The primitives hunted, just like animals that hunt, can we say that animals like to hunt? Or that they think of hunting as a duty? Monkeys and other mammals apparently can be in playing mode, I have actually seen them myself, some monkeys in Cambodia who were playing at jumping into the river from the trees, and a few meters away there were a bunch of little boys doing the same thing. Perhaps monkeys are getting dangerously close to modern humans. Lower vertebrates, like fish, are not known to engage in playing, as far as I know. We consider them inferior, although from another point of view they are doing better than we are, since they are not cursed in having to choose between duty and pleasure.

That's how I feel, perhaps by studying them so much, I mean fish, I have gotten closer to their way of seeing the world, a survival system that does not interpret events as duty or pleasure. Facts, and even memories, unravel themselves, what need is there to interpret them?

It seems like the passerine incident

It seems like the passerine incident that happened a few days ago may have inspired me. The bird was outside and wanted to inspect the world inside. I, who am inside, apparently made an attempt to inspect the world out there last night. It seems that last night while the Marshal was snoring, I got up and with the help of my crutches, I approached the window and opened it, a bit like Rita did when the passerine came in. Only this time it was to exit and not to enter. An exit, with on one side my hospital room and on the other the void, but apparently before the void there was this ledge. Piero found me on the ledge, I don't know how he did it, but he triggered the so-called alarm.

Alarm, patient on the run, or what else was it? Someone in your condition, Dr. Braglia scolded me this morning, someone in your condition, Pardini, what were you up to, a walk along the ledge? I hope you didn't want to jump, did you? he cut short. I didn't know what to answer.

To be honest, I don't remember what happened. What I remember is that while I was sleeping, I felt like I was stuck. I could hear the voices of people who want me to get out of the hospital, Karin, my mother, Malvezzi, Dr. Braglia, and at the same time

I felt this force that chains me down here in bed. And between these two equal and opposite forces there was me, stuck in the middle, and then like a bar of soap between two hands that goes *swish* and slips away, I slipped out of bed.

I wasn't quite flying through the air like a slippery bar of soap, I must say, but the direction towards the window was pretty clear, straight as an arrow like the Marshal says when describing a good play by the Rome captain. Straight as an arrow, I made it to the window, I remember this part quite well. How I got out, that I don't remember and I can't even explain it, all I know now is that my jump into the void was stopped by the ledge.

So? Dr. Bruglia insists. What's up with you, Pardini? Should we go ahead with a CHT? I wouldn't know, what is a CHT, exactly? I ask him. Compulsory Health Treatment, a procedure, the doctor tells me with an increasingly stern expression, applied in the case of a person suffering from a serious psychiatric condition that cannot be managed otherwise. But no, I tell him, Doctor, no, this condition is manageable, we can manage it, I'm sure, in fact, it's not even a condition. Pardini, he says, last night you were about to crash to the ground and break even the few unbroken bones that are left in you. And to bite the dust as well. Perhaps I suffer from sleepwalking? I tell him, looking for a loophole.

Dr. Broglia doesn't buy it. He looks at me like the teachers did at school when we came up with the most unlikely excuses to justify not having done our homework. He looks at my face as if looking for who knows what signs, perhaps all aspiring suicidal patients have particular features on their face that only doctors can detect. I can't bear his severe gaze, he knows it, and he insists, so I turn around, this Dr. Braglia is too strong for me. I hear his footsteps as he walks away. I call him back, I tell him Doctor, I'm sorry, Doctor. He comes back. Doctor, I, you know, tonight, maybe a nightmare, I tell him, I don't know. Of course, he tells me, of course Pardini, however, from now on the windows here will be sealed and only the nurses will be able to open them.

Of course, I say, it seems like a good . . . But I don't finish my sentence, as he looks at me as if I were trying to tell him how to do his job while instead I am just an aspiring suicidal patient, that's for sure. So, to wrap up our conversation, I tell him, Doctor, maybe last night's events could remain between us, I mean here, in the hospital, perhaps it would be better if my family didn't . . . Of course, Dr. Briglia tells me, and this is his first concession of today, of course Pardini, we won't say anything to your family, but stop acting silly.

He called me silly. He didn't beat around the bush, nor did he use psychiatric terminology for the patients' mental alterations and so on. Silly, that's what I had been. As Dr. Briglia walks away, I think back to last night, what got into me, if it was really a bad dream or an inevitable turn of events.

As I think about it, the stories of my father who had lived in the Libyan desert as a child come to mind. He had told us about this cruel game that he saw children play in Libya, when they found a desert scorpion. They put it on the sand, and then surrounded it with a curtain of fire all around, like a circular cage. At which point the scorpion was looking for an escape but could not find one. So what it did was position itself in the middle of the circle, it was as if it was looking at its tormentors, my father used to say, and while it looked at them, it committed suicide using its own stinger. Maybe it's just a legend, this story of the scorpion. Or my father's reconstruction. The thing is, in my case it gives you the idea.

Looking back

Looking back at last night's events, now I remember them a bit better. Maybe the effect of the medicines for my urinary infection is fading, and maybe it was the medicines that gave me the idea of getting out of here, to get some fresh air. Now I remember, I sat on the ledge, my legs dangling. One of my legs has a cast on it, so that one wouldn't be dangling much. I remember well that the moon was covered by some wispy clouds. I remember that the voices I heard before, in bed, were those of Malvezzi, of my mother, of Karin, while when I was there on the ledge, these voices were gone, swept away like wispy clouds too.

I don't really remember what I wanted to do. I can't remember if I really wanted to act silly or even jump off, as Dr. Braglia thinks. I guess I will never know. I will never be able to tell if I was an aspiring suicidal patient the other night. At best, I was an aspiring aspirant suicidal patient.

One thing I remember is that after a while I started talking, I don't know if I made any sounds, but anyways I was talking to myself. It was a three-way conversation, with my father who was explaining to me and Luisa why he had started studying physics at university. Luisa asked him questions and he answered, he made long speeches like I had never heard him do.

Too bad I can't remember them in detail, the things my father said. He was saying that he got interested in physics because he wanted to understand the secrets of the forces that move the world. What secrets? Luisa asked. They're secret, he replied, they cannot be explained, they have to be discovered. And how can I find them out? Luisa asked. Study physics too, my father said. We went on talking like that for a long time, I was mostly listening. The moon moved rather quickly, at least it seemed to me, and in the blink of an eye, it had ended up behind a hill, moved by the secret forces that my father was talking about.

While I was there looking for other stellar landmarks, I heard Piero yelling, and the sound of the alarm. Then I heard a whole bunch of people running, and I found myself surrounded by three thugs who took me by the arms, lifted me from the ledge and brought me back inside. That's all I remember for now. Then I went back to sleep, and the next day I found myself in front of Dr. Braglia who was scolding me.

Apparently Dr. Braglia

Apparently Dr. Braglia has kept his word. Both my mother and Karin came by this morning, and neither of them seemed to know anything about my walk on the ledge. They asked me about the fever, but no ledge. My mother also talked to the doctor, she said, that doctor of yours, he's on the ball, isn't he? I wouldn't mind a doctor like him. And the doctor didn't say anything to her, it seems.

Karin on the other hand kept talking about her friends on Facebook. About some pictures that a friend of hers had posted from Hawaii. Did you see Dr. Braglia, I asked her. Yes, she said, why? And what did he tell you? Nothing, he didn't tell me anything, he just greeted me. Well, I thought, good doctor. However, I bet the nurses know something. Of course, Piero must have told them. Rita has started to make jokes about my future participation in the Rio de Janeiro Olympics. Check it out, she said, how sporty our imaginary patient has become, what are you into these days, jumping the gun? Laura as always didn't say anything, but she also knew, you could tell from the way she smiled at Rita's jokes.

The only one who showed some compassion for an aspiring aspirant suicidal patient, of course, was Katia. She brought me a chamomile tea even though I hadn't asked her for anything, even after hours. Take it, she said, it will do you good. She didn't say anything else. A chamomile tea to calm my suicidal instincts, I guess. Surely, she had thought about it for a while, Katia never leaves anything to chance. She must have thought about my situation and must have decided that a chamomile tea was just what I needed. I have never liked chamomile all that much, but I drank all of Katia's. She even came to check from time to time. And so I drank, each time she showed up, down went a sip of chamomile.

Even April 28th has come to an end

Even April 28th has come to an end. Today I didn't do anything in particular. I didn't even look out the window, now I hardly think about the walk on the ledge any longer. I read a bit, as always, I also talked about soccer with the Marshal. I dozed off, because of certain new pills they give me that make me go to sleep. I also played a couple of hours with Lorenzo's DS. In the afternoon I tried to read the project that Schifano sent me the other day, but I couldn't do it, I will try again tomorrow. I was reading but wasn't really, that is, I slid over Schifano's words, like skates on ice.

Instead, a rather satisfying and noteworthy thing that I did, was take a good shit. I hadn't pooped well for a few days. I've only come down with some half-hearted shit, or difficult shit, or even aborted shit (yesterday).

Even today it didn't start out well. For starters, I had a hard time dragging myself to the bathroom and then getting into it, sitting down and setting down my crutches. It's not easy to take a shit in these conditions, it's not a natural thing, like when you do it without thinking much about it. When you are all broken into many pieces, so that you can hardly move, taking a shit becomes a big deal.

This in itself is not much of a problem. It's only a change of perspective. And then small things can lead to great problems but also to great satisfaction. To go back to taking my shit, I sat down and started out and it seemed like a complex affair, a tough fight like what had happened to me in the last few days. I also thought it was the continuation of the aborted shit from yesterday.

Instead, halfway through, everything went really smoothly. While the first half was, so to speak, uphill (it must have lasted at least five to ten minutes), the second half was gone in about twenty seconds. It was really very satisfying, smooth as oil and clean as water.

It's actually pretty rare, these days, that I produce such well done shit. Is it perhaps because of the spinach mound I ate the other day?

On my way back to my room, I was really satisfied. I felt lighter and more appeased, a physical sensation that merged with a psychological well-being. I remained in this state of mind for at least a good half hour, and indeed I think that afterwards, the rest of my day, even now that it's midnight, was influenced by having carried out such a successful shit. Well, goodnight now.

Today the feeling of well-being

Today the feeling of well-being derived from my successful shit has vanished. There won't be any more shit taking until tonight, so all I can do is read *Oblomov* for the third time. Besides, nobody will come to see me today, because they all went to my cousin Silvana's wedding. It's possible that Malvezzi will show up to check if I have read the project, but I hope not, because I haven't read the project yet, and I don't even know if I will read it today.

Is real life the one out there, where people go to my cousin Silvana's wedding, or is it this one in here, where aside from rereading *Oblomov*, the next stop, the next event will be tonight's shit? Is real life forgetting to live every day, or enjoying nothingness?

April 30th
Opened Schifano's project.

May 1st
Schifano's project put away. Is it Labor Day today or what?

Played all day with the DS. Headache.

I started working on Schifano's project

I started working on Schifano's project. I have the feeling that Malvezzi will come to see me soon. The deadline for submitting the project is in a few days, I'm sure Malvezzi will want to know where I'm at. Why the hell did I tell him to tell Schifano he could send me the project via email? What was I thinking? What came to my mind? Now I have to read the project during the Italian Cup final, with the Marshal who swears every time Totti the captain misses the ball.

The soccer game is over. Roma lost one to zero. Schifano wrote a nice project, I haven't finished reading it yet, but one can see it's a nice project. Totti was red-carded for kicking Balotelli. I don't know what Malvezzi is worried about. Schifano has put together a simple but very clear project, with all that is needed, the introduction, the expected results, the methodologies. There should have been a penalty for Roma.

Instead of Malvezzi

Instead of Malvezzi, Karin came to see me. I was pretty sure Malvezzi was going to show up, instead here comes Karin. Not only was she not Malvezzi but she was also in a hurry. She told me right away, she said I'm in a hurry, Monica is waiting for me, we're going for a coffee. Okay, I said, you're in a hurry. I came to bring you a book that I've just finished reading. Thanks, and what is this book about? It's not an intellectual and nihilistic book like these here, she said, taking a look at my two books *Oblomov* and *A Man Asleep*. These are not intellectual books, what does intellectual books mean? I asked her. Fine, you can think what you want, she told me. Then I asked her, and this book, which is not intellectual and nihilistic, what is this book about? It's the story of an American woman in crisis, she told me, who decides to go on a long journey to find herself, it's titled *Eat Pray Love*. Pray love? I asked her. Yes, that's it, the main character first goes to Italy, to eat, then to India to pray, and finally, to Bali where she falls in love.

So, in India she doesn't eat at all? No, not like that, I mean, every country has its own specialty, in Italy people eat, in India people pray and in Bali people love . . . whatever, it doesn't matter, I have to go now, if you're not interested I'll take it back. No, no, I said, leave it here, I'll take a look, leave it, c'mon. Okay, I'll leave it for you, she said, leaving the book on my bedside table. I waited for her to go away for real and then I took *Eat Pray Love* in my hands. It smelled good, especially the first part, where she goes to Italy.

In some kind of a prologue, the main character got separated from her husband who, however, is giving her a hard time because he does not want to grant her a divorce. Then in the end he grants it to her and so she, who in the meantime is with another guy, gives up the other guy too, and leaves for a long trip that includes Italy, India and Bali. I have not read it all, but from what I have read, in Italy she discovers the pleasure of food, in India prayer and in Bali she falls in love, but with a Brazilian not a Balian. There you go, eat, pray, love. At first glance, I would tend to agree, eat, okay, a vital function. Pray and love, I don't know. Pray what, love what, it's not clear. If you have to stick to three things to do, three vital functions, then I would say Eat, sleep, take a shit. *Eat, Sleep, Take a Shit* sounds like a nice title for a book. A book that deals with underestimated topics like sleeping and taking a shit.

People perhaps don't pay much attention to these issues, but when you happen to sleep badly, or shit badly, for example when traveling, when you're jet-lagged and cannot do things at the right time, or when you have your cast on and on crutches like me, you do realize the importance of sleeping and shitting properly.

People do talk about sleeping. but in the sense of dreaming, my dream is this or that. But sleeping per se, is not talked about much, for example in books. Nobody talks about sleeping in the sense of reaching the basal metabolic rate, I mean, taking into account only the essential energy expenses necessary for staying alive. On the other hand, when you wake up, you are active, your metabolism increases, so you have to eat, and if you eat, you digest, and your digestion increases your metabolism even more, so you can't take it anymore and that's why you get sleepy after a good meal. So, you might as well stay in bed.

What about taking a shit, who talks about that? Never seen a book or movie that talks about taking a shit in the title. Sure, about loves, defeats, crimes, passions, even eating like *The Big Feast*, but not *The Big Shit*. Yet everyone needs to take a shit once a day, sometimes even twice. For a good shit it can take ten, twenty minutes and I know people, Karin for example, who can also take thirty or forty minutes. Since we are awake about a thousand minutes a day, shitting is one to four percent of our day. A two-hundred-page book that wants to reproduce these proportions in a realistic way, should contain from two to eight pages dedicated to shitting. For example, a whole chapter, or diluted in several chapters, which would be even more realistic. The same goes for movies, a nice neo-realistic movie should show at least a couple of minutes of shit-taking. On the other hand, the only film I can remember in which people take a shit is surrealistic, by Buñuel.

I could also be wrong, I'm sure there are some exceptions as well. Come think of it, there are in fact whole books dedicated to pooping, but they're books for children. I found them in my niece Luisa's room and we read them together. Every time I went to see her we read them together. Our favorite is *Jacopòpò*, but I also love *Everyone Poops*, a booklet in English that shows a lot of animals that take a shit and also the shape of the poop, which I found very instructive since for those who study wild animals, poop is often the only source of data. One can use poop to figure out where the animals have passed by, to estimate their population density through complex formulas that take into account the number of shits per day and the time of deposition of the poop, and to infer their feeding habits. Animal poop is like an open window onto their daily life.

I remember that the university's zoology professor, in our first lesson, had drawn the general outline of an animal on the blackboard. A cylinder, crossed by a tunnel that passes the incoming food, and then the exit at the back of the cylinder. This, he said, is us, as well as all other animals. With a few exceptions, such as anemones, jellyfish and planarians, where the stuff enters and leaves from the same hole, but at different times. He added other details, Professor Limone—a strange name for a zoologist, the other professor's name was more appropriately Leo—said that the nervous system can be ventral or dorsal, the skeleton internal, external or absent. But as far as the tunnel goes, he said, there is no alternative, we all have it, from clams to snakes, from fish to humans. Food enters here, he showed with its stick, and leaves from there.

It was not so difficult

It was not so difficult to read Schifano's project. I think I may be able to work as a proofreader or something like that. Something that isn't engaging, something that has to do with other people's lives and not mine. So mine can stay at zero.

I remember when I was in Russia a few years ago, my friend Kostantin introduced me to Denis, a friend of his who works as a facilitator. Actually, first he started out as a dowser. One day, one of these new rich Russians called him to find water on the estate of his dacha. Denis went there with a friend of his who had some kind of a digging machine, and told him, Here, dig here. And everyone started digging and digging, but there was no water. Then he tried another hole, and another. After a dozen holes, he was fired and decided to give up dowsing. Instead, a field that looked very promising, Denis told us, was *facilitation*.

In Russia doing certain things can be very complicated, bureaucracy is much worse than in Italy. Each step takes its time, and sometimes it seems impossible to go through certain steps. I saw it for myself, the day after I arrived in St. Petersburg, Kostantin took me to the police station to report my arrival so that I could have a permit as a private visitor. And there, at the police station, we waited for hours while a man in his sixties was desperate in front of the commissioner. The commissioner was explaining—I didn't really understand what she was saying—but you could hear everything from outside the half-open door of the office, that she was trying to explain something and he, the more she explained, the more desperate he was.

That man stayed in the office for forty minutes, and eventually came out in tears. Kostantin then explained to me that what happened to that man was very common in today's Russia. They say that after the fall of the Berlin Wall, many things changed in Russia, the USSR disappeared, new states were created, there was some kind of total reset of the bureaucratic system. It turns out that if someone, like this desperate man, had lost his passport made before the reset, there is no longer any way to formalize who he is, where he was born, and all the rest of his history. In practice, the system created undocumented people who didn't know what to do with themselves anymore. There you go, these were all potential customers of Denis. He was helping people do things they couldn't easily do in today's Russia, where you need to get to know all the right people and know how to deal with the bureaucrat on duty.

Denis did everything by word of mouth, he told us, and besides, he wasn't really hired to solve problems. When he heard about a problem, he would simply start working to help solve it. If the problem was solved, usually those who had been helped, spontaneously repaid him in some way. For example, a ten-year-old girl needed to be operated on urgently, but with the Russian system this became a problem. Denis worked hard on this and managed to get her operated on in time. And the parents reciprocated in some way.

There you go, perhaps, if I get out of here one day, I would like to do something in the facilitating sector. Something that erases my person and my personal desires. But not a humanitarian thing, I don't know if I'm cut out for that. I would like to be a simple facilitator, even for small problems, other people's problems.

Schifano says in the project

Schifano says in the project on the effect of hypoxia, that the golden grey mullet of the Mediterranean lagoon areas, in conditions of hypoxia, is faced with a tradeoff. It can choose between (a) staying underwater, which biologists like Schifano call in the *water column*, risking dying of asphyxiation, or (b) emerging to breathe in the surface water layer which is rich in oxygen even when in the rest of the so-called *water column* the oxygen is missing, but risking being noticed by the cormorants and therefore, risking being eaten.

Schifano says that gregarious fish such as the golden grey mullet tend to synchronize their ascent to the water surface, they swim up in groups in order to minimize the risk of being caught by predators due to the evasive mechanisms of the school. It is well known, says Schifano, that gregarious fish exploit different evasive mechanisms that give them advantages over solitary fish. For example, the confusion effect.

The confusion effect caused by the shoal corresponds to a sensory saturation in the predator, so that a cormorant in front of a shoal of a hundred fish that skitter here and there, no longer knows which fish to catch. I'm saying this, not Schifano, but he implies it. Schifano then adds that it's all a question of balance, in terms of the choices of each individual fish. Even fish have a personality, there are those who are more courageous towards predators, and therefore take risks because their metabolism is high, they move a lot, they would immediately die asphyxiated if they stayed in the *water column*. There are quieter individuals who are also the most fearful, they stay where they are, so much so that they do not consume a lot of oxygen, and they can live in hypoxia for a long time, maybe even forever if there is at least a little bit of oxygen left in the *water column*.

The escape response is the last resource available to the golden grey mullet, if a predator attacks. The escape response is generated by two giant neurons which, being giants, allow for very short reaction times to escape predators. These giant neurons, Schifano says, send a signal to the anaerobic musculature which is superfast, while the aerobic one is slower but has more resistance. And that's also the case for humans, anaerobic musculature is what the Jamaican sprinters need to win the hundred meters while aerobic musculature is what the Kenyan runners need to win the marathon.

Schifano then says, given all this, that the last resource available to a fish when attacked by a predator is to use the escape response, i.e. their anaerobic musculature, then if it is anaerobic, whether there is oxygen or not, it shouldn't make any difference.

No, says Schifano, that is, maybe, says Schifano, we should look into this. It is true that a lack of oxygen in the water should not have an effect on the anaerobic musculature, as John Doe said in 1978, and then some other John said in 1986, but it is only a hypothesis, not proven. Instead, says Schifano, we have doubts. Don't the giant neurons that regulate escape responses, and the rest of the brain, need oxygen? And if there is no oxygen, won't everything just go down the drain?

We have to run some tests, says Schifano, who then got a bit caught up with the idea of developing a mathematical model that takes into account the dilemma between (a) going to the surface and making yourself visible to predators or (b) staying deep in these murky lagoon waters and therefore remaining invisible to cormorants, while at the same time also suffering negative effects to their flight response. However, I'd say that if the predators don't see the golden grey mullets in deep water, then they don't attack them either and if the golden grey mullets are not attacked, they won't need to flee.

What do you need the escape response for, if you are hiding? And staying, for as weird as it may sound, staying is also an escape. If everything around you is moving, the escape is accomplished by standing still. "A" moves away from "B" even if, seen from external observer "C", it could be "B" moving away from "A". "A" does something that "B" doesn't do, even if, again when seen from "C", in reality it is "B" that does something different from "A". Not doing something is a *doing* that is often underestimated. If one does not go to the cinema with friends who invite him, for example, he may think that he has missed an interesting experience. In reality, by not going to the cinema, one has acquired the experience of not having seen that film. Being here in this hospital, this ward, this room, I'm accumulating a lot of experiences of things I haven't done. Today, for example, in addition to not going to the cinema, I didn't drive my car, I didn't go to work, I didn't stop at the red light and then set off again at the green light, I didn't eat at the canteen, I didn't go to the supermarket on my way back, I didn't eat frozen pizza for dinner, I didn't feed the goldfish.

Today, I also had the experience of not talking to anyone. I just listened, to the Marshal who complained, Holy shit, are they ever gonna let me out of jail, to hell with them! he said, and then to Caterina who asked me if I needed anything else and I nodded no thanks, but I didn't say anything, and then to Dr. Bruglia who told me, We are almost there, Pardini, almost there. We're there, where? I thought, but I didn't say it.

Malvezzi came to see me tonight

Malvezzi came to see me tonight, as if he knew that in the end I would read the project, I bet this Malvezzi guy has a sixth sense. So, how's it going? he asked me, I know you're getting out. Not really, I told him, I'm not getting out, getting out to go where? Lapo, c'mon, Karin told me, you'll be out of here in a few days. If she says so, then why are you asking at all? In fact, I didn't ask you, Malvezzi told me. And he was right about that. So, I told him, You're right about this, but about the rest, not really. What rest? he asked me. The rest, I mean that I'm out of here in a few days, that rest is not a done deal.

Okay, it's not a done deal, he told me, but you're better, at least that's true. It's all relative, I told him, I'm better than three months ago but worse than six months ago. Let's forget it then, he says. Good, let's forget it, anyways, I know you came to see if I've read the project, then why don't you ask me right away? Well . . . I came to see how you were doing and then, also, if you had read the project, you know, Schifano cares a lot about it. So why doesn't *he* come to see me? He's not the hospital type, Schifano. I wasn't either, I told him, but now I'd stay here forever.

Fine, whatever, anyways, did you read the project in the end? he asks. Done. So? So, it's good, Schifano is a good writer, what do you want me to tell you, it's a good project. But is it okay? There must be something to change, to edit, isn't there?

What do you want to modify, Corrado, you know how things work at the ministry, so it's fine as it is, at best you could change the modeling a little. Change how? Just forget the mathematical model of the fish that go up and down with the metabolic functions and the fourth-degree equations and all that stuff. But then what do we put in there, Malvezzi asked, the predictive mathematical models are important otherwise the ministry will tell us that the project has no implications for management and so on and so forth . . . Then you could make a pictorial model, I told him. Pictorial? Pictorial, a beautiful pictorial model, I explained, with the golden grey mullet going up and the cormorant coming down to catch it on one side, and on the other, another golden grey mullet that hides in the deoxygenated turbid waters. Are you serious, Lapo? I guess we could make a PowerPoint diagram, huh? That could be a good idea, Lapo, because on the ministry website it says that explanatory files with schemes, diagrams etcetera can be added. You said *diagrams*, Corrado, I really meant *a pictorial model*, made by a painter, a carefully painted golden grey mullet, you could also paint whole fish schools that swim up and others that swim down, and flocks of cormorants, a Bosch kind of thing, or like a Diego Rivera mural, with all the details.

But wouldn't a diagram be easier, Lapo? Who is going to do the drawing for us? And then, the ministry website doesn't talk about drawings, only about diagrams. Do as you like, Corrado, I would do the pictorial model, but everything is fine with me, it's up to you, alright?

Look here, Lapo, today we had a meeting about job security, huh. Huh, you know what came out of it? That we can't work more than six hours a day at the computer, at the *terminal,* that's what they call the computer, the *terminal*, and then we have to take five-minute breaks every hour, huh, while instead so far everyone has been on their computers ten hours a day. The new director says that he will apply this rule. If not, it will be trouble, what do you say, Lapo? What do you want me to say, Corrado, I don't care, I don't spend eight hours on the computer, I don't even spend one hour on it, in fact some days I don't even turn it on.

Now you don't, said Malvezzi, because you're here on sick leave, but when you come back to work you'll have to use the computer, and you won't be able to exceed six hours. Of course, Corrado, I won't exceed six hours, you'll see, I won't. Malvezzi was happy, that for once I didn't tell him that I won't go back to work, he smiled, and he left happy.

Uncle Lapo, it would be nice

Uncle Lapo, it would be nice if mathematics existed, where when you do four plus four, you get forty-four, my niece Luisa told me today, while my brother Marco went to talk to Dr. Broglia. And what if you do six plus six, what do you get? I asked her. Easy, Luisa told me, it's sixty-six. And one plus two plus three? I asked her. That's a hundred and twenty-three, she told me. And one plus zero plus zero plus zero? A thousand. And eight minus two? Subtraction can't be done, she said. How come it can't be done? Nothing, sorry, it can't be done, you can only add, not subtract.

Then she asked me, Uncle Lapo, do you want to play Taboo? What's that? It's a game for guessing words, but without saying them. And can you play with only two people? Sure, we play with four, with my friends, but we can also play with two, she said, while looking at the Marshal who is sleeping on my left, and Lorenzo all concentrated on his little DS game, on the right.

And how does it work? Give me an example, I told her. I brought the cards, she told me. You're going to have to guess a word, wait a sec, I'm getting the cards. Here's an easy word, news-stand, let's say you have to guess *newsstand*, I will try to make you guess it, but I can't tell you these five words: kiosk, selling, tabloids, newspapers, magazines. Do you understand how it works?

I think I do, I told her. Show me how you do it. Okay, says Luisa, What's that thing with a person inside and you can go in and buy stickers . . . A newsstand! I told her. Good! She told me, although she knew very well that she had already told me it was a newsstand. Now let's do it for real, I said. Okay, Uncle Lapo, do you want to start? Sure, I'll start, I told her. Okay, Uncle Lapo, but let's do an easy one, something I can guess.

Of course, I told her, and I started looking at the cards. I'm sure a true Anglophile came up with this game, the first cards I saw were, in order, brunch, post-it, browser, broker, brief, DIY, blue jeans, bloody Mary, brainstorming, hashish, bug, all written in English, and Buddha—which in Italian is spelled Budda—and then open space, mouse, fringe benefit, frisbee, Forrest Gump, summit. Interesting words, I have to say.

Finally, I found Tortellini. The words I can't say are: Bolognese, ham, pasta, parmesan, broth. So, I tell Luisa, Okay, so it's something that you can eat as a first course, and you can eat it in a liquid . . . Minestrone! She said. No, no, but you're almost there, they're stuffed with meat too . . . Tortellini! Good girl, you guessed it! But that was easy, Luisa told me. Look, I told her, now your dad is coming back, why don't we play a game, he is going to have to say a word, like *hospital*, right, let's do *hospital*, but we can't say it, whoever makes him say it first, wins. Okay, she said, why don't you start, and then I'll talk to him too.

We remained silent, Luisa and I, with our secret, waiting for Marco, who soon arrived and said, So . . . Braglia said that you're doing much better, and that you're getting out soon, it's just a matter of days. Then I said, get out of where? Out of here, where do you want to get out of, Lapo, you've been here for months, soon you'll get out of here, and you'll be back with the living, out there!

Luisa looked at me with raised eyebrows, and said to her father, Dad, but where are we here? What do you mean, where are we? We're visiting your uncle, who had an accident, don't you remember? We often come here to see him, are you out of your mind, both of you? So I told him, and if we were out of our mind, where would they take us . . . ? To the madhouse, he said, I think you will really end up there, but what's going on, what is this silly game you're playing? I don't want to play these games . . .

C'mon dad, Luisa said, c'mon, one last question . . . Okay, sure, go ahead, ask me a question. So, Dad, if I break my arm, where will you take me? To the emergency room, but why should you break your arm? Then I asked him, Marco, but where is the emergency room located? It's downstairs, he said, on the ground floor!

Nothing, there was no way to make him say *hospital*. Luisa kept chuckling, and I kept asking him the silliest questions, like where did you do your internship? And he replied, in the cardiology ward, and then I asked him, where was Luisa born, Right here, he says, in the obstetrics ward. Look, he added, I don't want to waste my whole day with you guys in a silly hospital, which . . . Ha Ha Ha, you said it, you said it! We yelled at the same time. Said what? Hospital, you said hospital!

Last night I dreamed of my father

Last night I dreamed of my father walking down the street in the rain with a raincoat like the one Lieutenant Columbo used to wear. My father really had a raincoat like that and had worn it for years and years and I imagine that he still has it and that he wears it on the streets of Buenos Aires. My father walked and I followed him from above without showing up. At one point he stopped to ask for directions, but nobody understood what he was saying. I understood it from above but didn't want to interfere. He also didn't understand what they were saying but said thanks all the same. He was looking for something but could not find it. I knew what he was looking for but I couldn't tell him in the dream, it was as if someone had forbidden me. I remember that I knew what he was looking for, but I don't remember what he was looking for. I've been thinking about it all morning, but I can't remember what it was. I can clearly see the images of him walking, seen from above where I was, as if I were a camera fixed on a pole that followed my father.

I followed my father but I couldn't control what he was doing. They say that if you see your hands during a dream, you can control the dream. I saw my father's hands but I couldn't see mine so I couldn't control the dream. Then, while I was in semi-conscious sleep, other scenes with my father came to the surface, like that time when for my tenth birthday, I had asked for a ping-pong racket. We went into a shop to buy a rather special racket like a Stiga or something, and I had been as ashamed as a thief when my father said even if quietly, that if one knew how to play, a wooden scoop would have been just as good. That's what he said, word for word.

Then I saw again the scene of when I was staying at a friend's house one summer during high school and asked my father to bring me my electric guitar and I saw him coming to the gate with an electric guitar under his arm and I thought it was a very strange image, that of my father carrying an electric guitar, and it occurred to me that surely if one knew how to play well, a battered wooden guitar would have been just as good.

While I was semi-conscious, I also saw all my father's sandals that had gone through the summers of the seventies and eighties, one after the other. Especially a pair of German-style sandals, with two white buckles in front and one in the back, to close them. I don't know if he actually ever used the back buckles. I remember he always had them folded in front, so that the sandals could be slipped on and off more easily. He wore them for at least six or seven summers, because if one knew how to walk, those sandals were just as good for walking as any other pair.

I don't think my father was really attached to things, I think that he simply didn't buy anything new until he needed to, only that his threshold of need was very different than that of others. As a kid, I had rebelled a little against this attitude or was ashamed of it. Now, however, I think it's inevitable that I inherit this point of view, like some kind of a genetic disease that develops only at a later age, and one day it shows up out of the blue. Indeed, in addition to not wanting to buy new things, now I feel very light without old things. Things that I haven't seen here in the hospital for months, and therefore it's as if they no longer existed.

This morning I remembered that time

This morning I remembered that time I was about to go into the classroom, it must have been in first or second grade, I think that no one had fainted in class yet. I was going in and a bully from another class poked me from behind and said, Hey you. I turned around, and *Bam!* he punched me in the face.

I had never even spoken to him, I barely knew him and *Bam!* goes a punch in my face. I was stunned and then I went into the classroom. Marta, our teacher, was there, therefore we must have been in second grade. Marta was sweet and also pretty. She saw my black eye and asked me, What happened? And I said, Nothing at all, but then she gave me a big hug, and when she did that, I shivered and blushed.

Then she took me out of the classroom and took me by the hand and together hand in hand we walked through the whole corridor all the way to the director's office. To tell the truth, I don't remember the rest all that well. Most of all, I remember the corridor which was very long and I thought that before the end she would have let go of my hand and my chills would have stopped. Instead, she held my hand the whole time, until we got to the director's office, and then she held my hand there too.

Marta and the director asked me who did it but I didn't want to say. Marta looked at me as if to say that there was no need to be a hero, but I wasn't a hero, I just didn't want that kid to punch me in the face again. Then they found the kid who had punched me, I didn't say what his name was, but a little girl had seen everything and told her teacher. Marta then calmed down a bit and concentrated a little more on my eye, she said to me, But look what he did to you! And she took me to the nurse's office.

Still holding hands, and another very long corridor. There was a janitor in the nurse's office, but Marta wanted to do it herself. I didn't think I could withstand the additional chills caused by her eye care, but the eye hurt me badly so I let her do it. And she kept saying, But look at what they did to you, and now it was not a matter of a single bully, but of the whole world, what had they done to me, many of them, to me, me alone. Marta remained with us only for one year, the year of second grade. She didn't take me by the hand anymore, I guess because I didn't get any more punches in the face.

Today when I got back from physiotherapy

Today when I got back from physiotherapy, I found the bed made with one side of the sheets folded as a triangle, as if to facilitate the action of getting back to bed. Lorenzo and the Marshal were still doing their physiotherapy, their beds were made but without the triangle. Sometimes objects speak and this time the bed spoke, it told of Katia and of the care she had taken to make my bed and of the message that she had put in the triangle that she had made only for me. That triangle contained a clear message.

Sometimes objects speak, sometimes they say beautiful things, sometimes bad things, but they speak in the sense that they convey an intention. It is as if whoever did something in a certain way, like leaving the sheet folded with the triangle, had left an exclamation mark there, on the bed.

Like that artist who had made a Violin's Rage, which was represented by a destroyed violin, or like the time thieves opened my car in Marseilles, they had bent the door from above, at ninety degrees, though they didn't really steal anything because there was nothing to steal. But when you looked at it, it seemed like the representation of a Car Rape. The triangle left by Katia, on the other hand, could have been The Sweetness of the Sheet Folded by Hand.

I didn't dare go back to bed and wreck the triangle. I sat on the side of the bed for a while. Then I could hear Lorenzo and the Marshal coming, so I went to bed but being careful to keep the triangle in good condition.

The day went on without any other surprises. It wasn't Katia who brought me lunch, but Rita. Katia must have been busy. There is no predictable routine of who brings lunch or dinner, even if in the morning it's almost always Katia who makes the beds.

My mother came by in the evening, she seemed a little worried, I mean, more than usual. She started to beat around the bush a little bit. I went to the supermarket and I bought a nice piece of salmon ten euros, for Simone's birthday, and then some white wine, on sale for eight euros, then while I was at it, I also got five euros of caviar. And here what did they feed you today, she asked me, huh? As a first course, the first course, I told her, as a second, the second, and as a third, the third.

Then she started asking me if I had called Uncle Beppe, with his surgery. I know, I said, Sure you know, she said, but did you call him? I'll call him tomorrow, I said. And then please call this and that too, she added. But one could see that something was missing, because she was talking a bit too automatically, as if she were doing a task.

In fact, at some point, she said, but is it true that you are going to break up with Karin? Dunno, I told her, every time she comes here we fight, I don't know what she wants to do. She says it's you who treat her badly, Lapo, you tell her that you don't want to go home, but is it true, Lapo? Why are you doing this? I don't know if I treat her badly, maybe I treat her badly, but it's not that I don't want to go home. Aha, then you're going to go back home? I didn't say I'm going back home, it's that I want to stay here, and so the fact that I don't go home is a consequence of the fact that I'm staying here, it's not because I don't want to go home. Lapo, c'mon, stop talking nonsense, one day you'll have to get out of here, and then you'll have to go home. Perhaps, I told her, perhaps.

She seemed happy with that concession. Then she went back to talking about this and that, about the condominium meetings, she told me that at the last meeting the administrator had decided that the elevator expenses were to be shared equally, and I, she said, live on the first floor, but when do I take the elevator? Does that seem right to you? No. No what? No, it doesn't seem right, I told her. She looked quite surprised that I had expressed an opinion about her condominium affairs, in fact it just came out, I had not thought about it so much, I simply thought she asked me a question. Instead, my mother often puts question marks where there are no real questions and if one replies, she asks, what are you talking about? Well, she continued, this thing of the condominium is not fair, even the water, I don't know if I told you, but we share the water bills, can you believe that? What do you think I consume, in water? Basically, they drive me nuts, with their condominium meetings. Anyways, now I have to go, I'm going to pick up Luisa from school, and please call Uncle Beppe, how many times do I have to tell you, she said.

Actually, I don't want to get out

Actually, I don't want to get out. The more I think about it, the more I don't want to get out. So, I also stopped thinking about it, because it is now established that I don't want to get out. I was offered this opportunity on a silver platter, the opportunity to withdraw, and I would like to seize it.

There is like a background noise in life out there, of which I sense the memory. It's like one of those noises that you only notice when they stop, like when you are in the kitchen reading and don't notice any noise, then suddenly the refrigerator goes silent and you realize, in retrospect, that while you were reading the fridge was actually making noise, some kind of low frequency vibration. Now that I am here in the hospital, I realize what it was, that background noise around me when I was out. Which, however, being a background noise is imperceptible when you are in the middle of it. That background noise that makes you accept that we now have mobile phones, GPS in the car, racing bikes with racing bike shoes, the iPad and the iPod, the television always on, the TV shows where people pretend to pretend.

Here, after all, from this hospital point of view, these things hardly exist. Even the DS is gone, I gave it back to Lorenzo, that thing gave me a headache. What's left are the walls, the ceiling, the sound of nurses walking in the distance, Dr. Scholl's clogs all around me, Katia's ankles, the Marshal's snoring noises, a couple of books on the bedside table, and the memories that come back to me every now and again and stick to the stains on the ceiling.

A memory that came back to me today and with which I fiddled a lot is that of Teacher Elisa who shot a three pointer once with my notebook. I was in first grade, I hadn't thought up my heroic act to save Caterina Magri yet, although I think I had already noticed her because of her jeans with colored patches. I was doing well at school, we were all doing well, it seemed to me, we all got nines and tens, but every now and then someone would do something wrong, like use the wrong color, or the wrong proportion in a drawing. Then it was all seven-double minuses across the page. Once it happened to me too. I can't even remember what I did wrong. What I do remember, is that Teacher Elisa called me to her desk and started to mark my notebook with red marks, and that she wrote *seven-double-minus* on it. That was painful enough, but it was not over yet. Teacher Elisa then took the notebook as if it were burning or as if there were spiders in it or whatever, as if she had to get rid of it as soon as possible, and she threw it away. The launch lasted quite a while and I was granted plenty of time to savor the worst defeat, like an insult added to the injury. The notebook arced like a three-pointer and went straight into the trash bin, without even needing to bounce off the wall. I had to go get it among the banana peels left by some other kids during the mid-morning break. That was perhaps the first time that I got to see with my very own eyes one of those mocking coincidences that actually happen quite often.

Perhaps because it's from so long ago it's a memory that I like, when I think about it, especially the three pointer. What did Teacher Elisa think when she made the three pointer? I don't remember her always shooting three pointers with the other kids' notebooks, or certainly not every single time. There were at least seven or eight meters between her chair and the trash bin, which was next to the door. In addition, notebooks are not like basketballs, notebooks open and close, the pages flutter changing the air resistance, so each shot has its own pattern. In that shot, one could feel a sense of inevitability that started as soon as I saw that the teacher had thrown the notebook in the direction of the basket, even if she had thrown it without looking. And actually, it was especially because she had thrown the notebook without looking. That sense of inevitability that you feel when, for example, you get a ticket the only time you park your car in an illegal spot for ten minutes, a kind of Murphy's law that comes upon us and that in a way, we have sought out.

And this, like the other memories that come back to me, is a beautiful fresh memory, never used before. It's not like one of those memories remembered many other times so you never really know if you remember the memory as such, or the memory worn out from all the other times you remembered it. Nope, really, I had never remembered this three-pointer memory before. It must be due to the effects of the third-degree retrograde mnemonic deficit that I had, maybe. I don't know. I just know that I don't even have to make an effort to go and look into my mind for these episodes that are over thirty years old, they come to me on their own, as fresh as newly laid eggs.

This morning I heard that Rita was asking

This morning I heard that Rita was asking Katia, Caterina where were you hiding? But why did she call her Caterina? Wasn't her name Katia? Don't pull my leg with these jokes, please. I always get confused with names, but Katia? C'mon, I'm pretty sure her name is Katia.

Then Karin showed up. My books, I said, you could give them away. And who do I give them to, she asked me. Give them to the library. Don't you have a friend who works at the library? Monica. Okay, Monica, ask Monica if we can give them to the library. So, if I ever want to, I can also go and read them again.

Okay, I'll ask her, she said. But if you can go and re-read them, does that mean that one day you will get out of here? I will, I said. When? One day, you said it yourself, I told her. And when will this blessed day be? I can't answer this part. Lapo, she said, you've been here for four months, are you going to take root? I like it here, I told her.

I don't know, she said, maybe it's better if I move out. But why would you move out? I asked her. It's just that we always fight. But why would moving out make a difference? So that we don't fight anymore. Not true, I told her, if you don't want to fight anymore, don't come to see me anymore, but you don't need to move out. You can stay home, I'll stay here, and if you want to fight, you can come to see me. If you don't want to fight, don't come to see me, what's the problem? What a smart idea, she told me, great, then I'll stay home and you stay here. Right, I said. For good, she replied. That would be great, I said.

Today I got this idea

Today I got this idea: that Katia is none other than Caterina Magri! First of all, her name is Caterina, not Katia. She calls herself Katia to make it easier for everybody, I'm sure, because both Rita and Piero call her Caterina. Or Cate. That must be where the name Katia comes from. The letter *K* then has nothing to do with it, I added it by mistake. Furthermore, she is about my age, so if she is my age now, she was my age even when I was seven years old and I wanted to save her when she was going to faint. Obviously, she never fainted because it didn't suit a future nurse. If anything, she would be the one who saved people who fainted, not the other way around.

I need to find out her surname, although it may not matter because maybe she got married and changed her name, even if she was Magri as a girl. Now her name may have become Marcuzzi or Malvezzi if she had married Malvezzi, which would never have happened, knowing her. I don't know if Catherina knows what my first and last names are, and even if she does, she doesn't necessarily remember them. Or does she? Maybe that's why she puts so much effort in making my bed! It could be that she knows who I am but thinks that I don't know who she is. Okay, I don't know, I'm not sure as of now, and before I had never even thought about it. But it is also true that before, when I had never thought about it, I shivered when she made my bed or when I looked at her Dr. Scholl's ankles or I looked at her hands or anything else she did, I always shivered. And is this not a major coincidence? They say that dogs recognize their owners from their odor even if they haven't seen or heard them for a whole year or for a bunch of years. The memory of the nose remains and they recognize the owner. Even I, perhaps I think in one way with my brain, while with my nose, leading to the chills, I think in another way. That is, in the way I recognize Caterina Magri, that's why I shiver in her presence.

Her hair is brown and what was Caterina Magri's hair like? Brown! Everything else is also the right color. The similarity is there, for sure, there is no doubt about the similarity. And the town, it's the same town. It was I who had moved and then lived here and there, only to return to these parts a couple of years ago. But Caterina must surely have stayed in this town, she must have enrolled at the nursing school. And it's pretty normal that if you go to nursing school, then you will end up becoming a nurse. It all makes a lot of sense.

I have to come up with a plan, a simple plan to figure things out now. I mean, I have figured it out, she is Caterina Magri, that goes without saying. But let's lay all the cards on the table, that's the best way to go about it. Who shows their cards first? Me or Caterina? Better if I let her do it, so I have a little advantage. When she comes to make my bed tomorrow, I could tell her, So are you going to lay your cards on the table? I don't know how it's done here in this world, or around here in this hospital, with this kind of things. Maybe I would end up scaring her and that's not a good idea, I need to be very careful with her. One shouldn't get too personal with the nurses. Though it's Rita who always makes fun of me, she gets kind of personal with me. Rita, the wrong one. I need to find a very delicate way to get to the point, by showing my cards. If I overdo it, then the magic is over. Perhaps even the chills will end if the cards are shown too early. Better to leave everything between the "said" and the "unsaid".

You know that she knows that I know. Or, I know that you know that I know, and it's better to keep it between us.

Let's assume, for now, that she knows. That would explain why she dedicates all this attention to me. Now that I also know, what's missing? She knows, I know, but she doesn't know that I know, even though I know that she knows. Here's what's missing, she doesn't know that I know, and she doesn't even know that I know that she knows. I have to let her know, but very carefully. I have to tell her somehow, maybe indirectly. These things are delicate. These things happen spontaneously. One must be careful not to overdo it, overdoing it is wrong. One has to be careful not to scare her away, she may end up changing hospital wards, if she gets scared. Maybe her husband, if she has a husband, will be the one who makes her change wards if he finds out that she has tracked down an old flame of hers. One has to be very careful, one can easily make mistakes about these things. People get scared for a lot less.

Saying and not saying

Saying and not saying, sometimes people think about it too much when it's not necessary, people understand each other very well, and there is no need to say much. And sometime people misunderstand you if you say anything at all. As for Caterina, I don't know what to tell her, maybe it is better if I don't tell her anything, we may understand each other better that way. Even seeing and not seeing, there too, you never know what is better, and whatever you see is not necessarily what is really happening. Or you see dreams that are not real but you then see them as if they were.

Sometimes what you see with your eyes doesn't stick around, while what you imagine is easier to remember well even if you haven't really seen it. I remember once at a congress, one of the first congresses on fish that I ever attended. Ichthyologists still talk about it. On the last day of the congress, a skinny guy with messy hair came up on the stage. He was supposed to give a presentation about the fish of the Amazon River. He immediately apologized, he said I'm sorry, but, well . . . I came by plane, I put my presentation slides in my suitcase, and my suitcase has not arrived yet. I have been waiting for it for three days.

So we all thought, now he is going to step down and we'll go straight to the next presentation. Instead, he stayed there and said, So, I'm going to give my presentation anyways but with virtual slides, please concentrate, I'm going to show them all to you now.

This is the first slide, that's the title of the presentation, that is, *The escape response of angelfish from the Amazon*, he said, and underneath is my name and that of my colleagues. Next slide, this is an angelfish, you can see the yellow color with black stripes, you can see the discoid body and the pectoral fins with lateral insertion, all of these features ensure that it has excellent maneuvering ability.

Next slide, here is the natural habitat of the angelfish, the Amazon River, you can see the vegetation, the dark-green long-leaf phanerogams in the water that create a structurally complex environment where fish need high maneuverability.

At each new slide he said *Next,* like everyone else did at every change of slide by turning to the technician who was operating the projector. But he actually spoke with his eyes lost in the air as if to announce that he would move on to the next slide. He was also holding a stick to indicate the details of each slide on the screen. And he went on like this, one slide after another, describing them all to us. And the beauty of it is that we really saw them, because of the effort and attention we invested in creating images from his descriptions, we were all listening very carefully, no one missed a single word, I remember that presentation better than any other, even better than my own.

At the end, after a standing ovation from everyone, he asked, Are there any questions? And someone from the audience, a Canadian guy with sideburns and a mustache, said, Yes, I have a question, could you put the third slide back? And he, after looking at the screen for a few seconds, said, This one? No, the one before, said the Canadian guy. Then this one? Yes, said Dr Sideburns, there you go, I wanted to ask you, how did you manage to film in those turbid conditions?

For the last few days

For the last few days I have been getting a headache in the evening. It's not because of the DS, that can't be, because I gave it back to Lorenzo. It's like during the day I read and then in the evening I have a headache. Dr. Briglia, my brother Marco and, while she was at it, my mother as well, all told me, You need glasses, you get to a certain age and then you need glasses.

I told them, but what age are you talking about, what is it, is there a specific age at which one needs glasses? And then, what kind of glasses? Everyone has an age, Dr. Braglia told me, and Marco agreed. And at that age, they told me, you need glasses. I can see very well, I replied, and I read very well, what glasses are you talking about?

But in the evening you do get a headache, don't you? they told me, and I'm sure they are just ganging up on me, without my knowledge. Okay, well let's say I need glasses. But then what did the primitives do, since they hadn't invented glasses yet? What do the primitives have to do with it? they told me in unison, and then they added, Sure, there were no glasses, but there weren't even books to read.

Maybe there weren't any books, but there were rock inscriptions and then there were needles to insert in leather, to make clothes against the glaciations. This too has nothing to do with the whole thing, they said, especially my brother, but also the others, since they are all ganging up on me. First of all, it was the young women who sewed the skins, said Marco, and then the rock inscriptions are drawn quite big, they can be seen from two meters away.

But then came the Egyptians with their papyri and the Romans with their milestones, and nobody wore glasses, I said. Okay, whatever, are we talking about prehistory or about healing your headache? they asked me. About healing my headache, I told them. But glasses are not natural, that's why I don't want to wear them. I like natural things, like the primitives and also all the ancient civilizations, at least until the discovery of glasses, when things were going just fine as far as I know. Great, Marco retaliated, you like it natural . . . then what about books? Books are not natural, they certainly don't grow on book-plants, yet you read them, don't you?

Holy shingles, you're right, I told him, about this, you're right but what can I do, even if you're right. I read books anyways, even if they are not natural. However, I don't like glasses at all, they bother me and then they are not natural, even if, on this point, I admit that you got me. So you'll have to live with it, with your headache, they told me.

And so I have to live with my headaches. I get one a day, usually around dinner time. During the day I read and then in the evening, here comes my headache. If I don't read, sometimes I get it anyways so there goes their theory about books causing my headache. Then I might as well read, at any rate it's always the same books that I am re-reading so I don't even need to read word by word. I just need to know what chapter we are in, and words come to me even without reading them.

And then I could ask Caterina to bring me some carrots, apparently they are good for improving your vision. I am sure that if I ask her, she will bring me a bushel of carrots.

I feel like I'm running out of oxygen

I feel like I'm running out of oxygen, with this thing that everyone wants me to get out of here but me. Dr. Bruglia even gave me a day, he told me *Thursday*. He didn't say anything else, all he said was *Thursday*, but I know what he was referring to, he was referring to the day I will have to get out. The others, including my mother, Marco, and Simone, also talk to me as if I will be out soon, they are already inviting me to their houses for the weekend, since I'll be out of here on Thursday, according to them. Instead, I feel like I'm running out of oxygen, with this thing of getting out. Maybe also because it's so stuffy in this hospital. It could be that, too. But if it were that, then I would have run out of oxygen even before, in all the weeks I've spent here. Instead it's only been the last few days that I've felt like I'm running out of oxygen, ever since Dr. Braglia told me *Thursday*.

I don't know what to do, I'm running out of oxygen. I feel like screaming *I'm running out of oxygen!* But then I feel ashamed, since Caterina could hear me. These are the disadvantages of having a former schoolmate as a nurse, with whom there's a relationship that goes beyond mere camaraderie. If there were regular strangers or even just Piero, Laura and Rita, I wouldn't have any inhibitions, I would shout *I'm running out of oxygen!* But there's Caterina, so I am stuck with my lack of oxygen.

I also asked the Marshal, he replied, Running out of what? Oxygen, I told him. Geez, he told me, C'mon Lapo, we're in a friggin' hospital, where did you think you were? Up in the mountains, open air, with the friggin' birds chirping around you? Of course, you're running out of oxygen, Lapo, we've been in this fuckin' hospital forever! Screw them!

Whatever. I can't make it, every breath is a major struggle to get my oxygen, I feel I'm running out, I feel like I may faint. It would be ironic, I mean fainting, with Caterina helping me, while instead it was me, several decades ago, who came up with the idea of helping her one day when she was going to faint. For the last couple of days, my every breath has not been natural, it is something that requires a major effort. Here's a breath, here's another one, a third one. It's like I'm counting them, as if I had only a limited number of them available, before having to pass out permanently. I can't go on like this, I can't even sleep.

Fish, when they lack oxygen, have two strategies, each species has its own. What makes sense when oxygen is lacking, is to do as cod do and decrease activity. This way, cod reduce their energy needs to a minimum and therefore also reduce their oxygen consumption. Then they wait. They wait for the oxygen level to rise, otherwise sooner or later they'll crash. This is what all somewhat sedentary, basically lazy, species do. If they lack oxygen, they become even lazier. Other species like herring, which are much more active, swim all the time in the open sea, and that's another strategy. If by chance they are in areas with little oxygen, because the bottom currents are remixing or because they are part of a school so large that the other fish consume all the oxygen, the herrings increase their activity, that is, they swim faster. Which does not seem to make much sense because it makes them consume even more oxygen. However, increasing activity makes sense for herring, and that sense lies in getting out of there.

In the end I got out

In the end I got out on Thursday, I wouldn't have done it but I gave up in the end, it's not like I had a lot of choice. Piero the nurse came, with Gustavo the physiotherapist and Dr. Broglio, while Caterina was standing on one side, looking at me. Dr. Bruglia said, Pardini, today is D-day, is everything ready? Is anyone going to pick you up? Yes, everything's ready, I told him, and, No, no one is coming to pick me up, I will take a taxi.

Simone, Marco, Karin and my mother all knew I would get out, but I broke up with Karin, at least temporarily she says, my mother went to Simone's since it's my niece Luisa's first communion, and therefore also Simone and Marco cannot come. Just as well, I thought, I didn't really want to go back into the world, but if I really had to do it, at least it was better to do it alone. That is, by taxi. As far as walking, I am managing quite well, with two crutches, sometimes even with one. Guglielmo helped me, even Caterina did her part. To be honest I didn't need her help, but when Caterina approached me I let her. She had her left arm around me, which caused me asymmetrical chills all over my body, as I tried not to step on her Dr. Scholl's clogs and not to trip over her tapered ankles. On the other side, Girolamo was holding me for real, so I was walking all wrong, much worse than what I would have done if left alone, in fact Dr. Broglia said to me, Pardini, c'mon, you can do it, you don't need any help!

That frigging doctor was right, Guglielmo and Caterina looked at him as if they were saying, Should we let him go? And he nodded, so suddenly I was on my own. The first one to dump me was Gustavo, then I looked at Caterina who was a bit hesitant. But in the end the doctor looked at her so she dumped me, too.

Like a blender with the plug disconnected, the chills I felt on my left stopped, and I started walking along the corridors of the hospital. Caterina went to call a taxi while Gerolamo brought me my suitcase. I had never left a hospital after spending four months in it. There was an incredible light outside, you couldn't even open your eyes if you didn't want to be blinded. As the light crushed me, a whiff of the Italian spring came to me that stunned me. I had already been knocked out by the Italian spring, many years ago. Coming back to Italy after several years abroad, I had landed in Milan Linate of all places, and yet Milan Linate was good enough for me to get a whiff of the Italian spring as I walked down the airplane steps. They say that scents are the most hidden thing that goes straight to the subconscious, much more than vision, and in fact these whiffs of the Italian spring stun me. It has also happened to me elsewhere, especially when I've returned to a place where I have previously lived. For example in

Scotland, where I lived for two years. Once I went back, I got a scent of the Scottish low tide. But there's nothing like the whiff of your motherland. Not that I'm a nationalist, but the whiff of your motherland is the one that touches you in the same neurons as when you were a child. In my opinion, every country, maybe even every region, but I would say above all every country has its own whiff chemistry. In Italy, the whiff is perceived especially in the spring, and must be composed of different pollens, I imagine, but also of the smell of coffee and paved Italian streets and a mixture of the leftovers of Italian lunches and dinners.

I waited for a couple of minutes in the middle of the Italian spring, then a taxi arrived, Caterina said goodbye, what was I expecting, a hug? The hug did not come. She just said goodbye, Mr. Pardini, she called me. I didn't know what to say. I wanted to say something about the fact that I had not been able to save her in elementary school when she fainted, but then I remembered that she had never fainted, that's why I never saved her, so I didn't say anything. I looked at her, I looked at her Dr. Scholl's clogs, and I got into the taxi. I never thought it would go this way, leaving the hospital.

I got home, the house is almost empty. Karin took all her stuff, which is a lot of stuff. There is still the bed, a table, four chairs and a wardrobe with my clothes. An armchair, a sofa and a television on a coffee table. I'm back to the world of the living, now what do I do? Tomorrow I have to go to work, but today what do I do? I sat in the armchair and looked up in the air. The ceiling is very different from the one we had in the hospital. Everything is different around me, but in reality, or perhaps for this very reason, the only comparison, the only thing a bit equivalent and therefore comparable, is the ceiling itself. In the hospital, there were dots spread around some gray spots in each of the four corners, and paths could be made by joining the dots in lines surrounded by gray spots. Here instead, the ceiling is very white, no path for the dots, and even the dots are too few. At best, all I get is a broken line with obtuse angles, nothing like a nice, sinuous path. I look at the ceiling and the images of the hospital ceiling flow in front of me. Then I seem to hear hospital noises, and among these noises, the sound of footsteps, I also see Dr. Scholl' clogs, those of Caterina. Instead, it's my neighbor's footsteps that I hear.

I'm starting to get hungry

I'm starting to get hungry, but I am no longer used to eating by myself, everything was much simpler at the hospital. Here, instead, I have to feed myself. The fridge is empty and it's no wonder, Karin has taken everything away, there are only tuna cans left. Luckily, there is a little pasta so I make rigatoni with tuna which I throw in a saucepan, after browning a piece of dried garlic. This makes me think of my father, when we used to go back to the city in the summer while my mother stayed at the seaside. My father worked throughout the week and I had to take some university exams. He always used to eat like this, heating up some tuna or peeled tomatoes without many condiments, and then we would make spaghetti.

He couldn't do without wine, it was one of the few things he couldn't do without, wine with meals, and cigarettes. The wine, however, often wasn't there because there was no way he would remember to go grocery shopping. I studied all day and when he came back it was always too late, the shops were closed. At home, there were only aged and precious Baroli and Brunelli di Montalcino, given to us as gifts on the occasion of important anniversaries by relatives who had mostly disappeared or lived far away. Some of these wines my father had in fact opened and finished, during his summer returns to the city when he found himself short of wine for dinner, but this behavior was discovered later by my mother, and therefore my father had changed strategy.

Then, he said to me, look, now I'm going to do like Jesus did at the wedding at Cana. He filled some glasses with tap water. Watch this, he said, as he went into the living room to look for liquors. He returned with a bottle of Glen Grant. With an eighty-proof whisky, he told me, just dilute a glass of it with three and a half glasses of water. Here you go, he showed me, while he carefully poured the glasses one by one into a pitcher, first those with water then the one with whisky, as if preparing a chemical reaction. Then you mix well, he said, so as to achieve the gradation of the wine uniformly. That was how he made wine, my father, like Jesus.

Then we would sit at the kitchen table and have dinner. I would have the spaghetti on my plate, and a glass full of tap water. My father would hold the saucepan with his left hand with the rest of the spaghetti in it, and the fork with the right. Meanwhile, he would sip his Canaan wine from time to time, and wink, as if to say that I was missing out.

Cigarettes were the other thing

Cigarettes were the other thing my father couldn't give up. Sometimes on Sunday evenings he found himself without cigarettes, and the tobacco shops were closed. I remember once, I must have been six or seven, and a fairground had been installed near our house for a few days. That Sunday afternoon my father told my mother, I'm going to take Lapo to the fair. My mother looked at him like that was odd, usually he didn't take this kind of initiative.

I got dressed in a hat and coat, it was very cold, we must have been in the middle of the winter. My father took me by the hand and together we followed the lights of the fair that were flashing at the end of the avenue. I had never even asked my parents to go to a fair, I was also a little amazed, but I held my father's hand tight and I thought about what I could do at the fair.

My father bought me some cotton candy, we shared a piece of nougat, I shot some cans and I won a puppet with an Inter-Milan shirt. At that point, that is, once I had won the Inter-Milan puppet, my father changed gears and started looking for the miraculous fishin' machines, that's what he called it, *miraculous fishin'*. There are always, he said, these machines in the fairs. I also started looking with him left and right, in all the corners of the fair, and in the end we found them behind the roller coaster. They were two large transparent containers, one next to the other, both full of assorted objects. They worked with the golden fair tokens. You put a token inside, and then there was a sort of crane to operate. At one of the machines there was already a freckled boy with his mother watching him. We started to watch, too. With a token, you got only one move to operate the crane, lower it onto the objects, grab one with the teeth of the crane, and then bring it back up so that the object would come out of a hole. It didn't seem easy at all. The freckled kid almost always grabbed a red Ferrari model, but as soon as he tried to pull it up, the Ferrari dropped from the crane.

We studied it for a while, then my father went to the cashier and bought a handful of golden tokens and told me, Let's make sure we win, and if we have more tokens left, you can use them on the rides. We went back to the miraculous fishin' machines. My father started tinkering with the crane. Half-hidden, in the midst of all the dolls, toy cars, balls and stuffed toys, there were a couple of Diana cigarette packs. That's what had prompted him to take me to the fairground, even if he had restrained himself at the beginning, in order to let me do everything a boy should do at the amusement park first. He had done his duty as a father, and now he was standing there concentrating on grabbing a pack of Diana cigarettes, next to the boy who was spending a fortune on that red toy car.

After several attempts and ever new strategies, my father finally managed to win a pack of Diana's. It had been inexplicably suspended between two teeth of the crane and my father managed to put it in that strange position right above the hole. He had to use the last token, and I was really cold, so I told my father I wanted to go home. He went behind a pole to light a cigarette, and then took me by the hand. I don't really like Diana's, he said on the way back, they don't taste like much.

I slept on the sofa

I slept on the sofa with the television on but without volume. The images were still going when I woke up, it must have been six in the morning. I dragged myself down the corridor, without crutches, to get to the bathroom and take a shower, but the water was cold. I took a cold shower that woke me up and reminded me that today is the day I have to go back to work.

While I was having breakfast, my mother called, she was all worried, she'd been looking for me all day. I told her, But I just got up! And she said, All day I meant yesterday. Then she told me about my niece Luisa's communion. Uncle Beppe was there and it turned out that I had never called him, Call him, she said, do you have the number or you want me to give it to you again? I have it, I told her. Mmm, she told me, and then she hung up, she had to swing by the neighbors because of the condominium meeting.

Meanwhile, I'm thinking that I can't go back to work, I can't do it, yet I have to. I guess I will be sending someone else who is not me. I guess it's like I'm staying here. I am going to leave my brain here, well wrapped and in a drawer, and I'll get it back when I come back. Here I go.

Taking the bus is not a simple thing if you have crutches. Using crutches seems like no big deal but it makes you understand how the world is made for those who don't use them. Finally, I sit down, look out the window and see tree-lined avenues that I don't remember, I see kids on the street whom I don't remember. There are also some stray cats that I don't remember, they must have been born in the months that I was in the hospital. There are a lot of things that I don't remember seeing before.

Anyway, on the bus nobody asks me, Are you back? While I'm afraid that at work they will say that. I don't want to be back, but even if I'm back, at least I don't want to be told. Like someone who comes last in a race, they don't like being told over and over, You came last, they know it very well, they got to the finish line, nobody was behind them, so they were last, there is no need to go tell them. I look at the tree-lined avenues that were not there before and it occurs to me that I could come up with a plan. A plan that starts today and takes me far.

I think about it, and my father comes to mind, feeding pigeons in the squares of Buenos Aires. He's wearing his Lieutenant Colombo raincoat and that makes me smile because of the association between the *Columba livia* pigeons of the square and Columbo the lieutenant, which occurs to me for the first time. I also think that I could visit my father soon, and that he wouldn't ask me many questions like *you're back*, and that maybe we wouldn't talk to each other much at all. Only a few monosyllables would be sufficient.

When I get to work, then, so as not to get noticed, I could go in through the back door, wait for people to be in the coffee room, and then go into my office trying not to use my noisy *cling clang* crutches. Then I could call the secretary without leaving the office and tell her that I came back. Then I could call Rome, the central office, and inquire about how to take a sabbatical year or something. Finally, I could send a message to my friend Armando, who works in Rio Claro, southern Brazil, and ask him if he has room in his laboratory. I could visit him for six months, or even a year. That way I can also visit my father in Buenos Aires every now and then.

I arrive at work. I go in through the back door. I go upstairs and hear footsteps of people going to the coffee room. I also hear Malvezzi's voice, he's speaking with Schifano. The secretary is talking to the director. Everyone is in there. So I go the other way, I go in my office and close the door. My office is exactly how I left it. Stacks of sheets and articles that I can no longer tidy up, several stacks are on the ground because there is no longer a place on the desk. Boxes are still closed from previous moves. It's difficult to move around in this office on crutches.

I manage to sit down and call Rome, the central office. Mrs. Scozzafava replies. I am a researcher at the Ecosystem Center, I tell her, I would like to know if it is possible to spend a period at a foreign university. Mrs. Scozzafava doesn't seem to understand, she says, but are you going on a scientific mission? No, I tell her, it's not really a mission, I mean a long period, six months or a year. Oh, she says, then it's another thing. Another thing compared to what, I think, but I don't tell her. So, would it be possible? I insist. You need to have a host institution, she tells me, and then you can ask for a leave of absence from your institute's director and also from the head of your research unit. How long are you going for? A year, I tell her, I would go for a year. Would you go on leave, or on salaried leave? Salaried, preferably, Then you must download form xx and then also form xy.

So I can leave. Although I will have to ask the director and the head of my research unit for a couple of signatures, and it will not be easy. The best thing would be for Armando to send me an invitation, so that I can take the invitation to the director and tell them that I have been invited. I would like to go, if it's possible, I'll tell them, so it'll look like leaving wasn't my idea.

I think I won't call the secretary. I did sign in at the entrance, anyways. Hopefully nobody will notice. I write a message to Armando, to ask him if he would host me in his laboratory for a year, if he has room for me. Armando is a hypoxia expert, we could do some good work together. And then staying in the other hemisphere could do me some good, there are different perspectives down there. As long as Guglielmo lets me go. I should do a couple of months of physiotherapy at day hospital, but I would like to leave as soon as possible.

Armando, I ask him via Skype, are you there? Armando? He replies almost immediately. Listen, Armando, I tell him, those experiments on hypoxia along the coast, do you still have plans to do them? Yes, but how are you, he says, weren't you in the hospital? I'm out, I'm fine and I would like to come to see you, what do you say? At the end of June I'm going to the Pantanal jungle, he tells me, to work on hypoxia in the pools of the Rio Miranda. In the Pantanal? I ask him. Yes Lapo, he tells me, in the Pantanal there is a swamp especially during the rainy season, from November to April. Then everything dries up, and all you have is the river and some isolated ponds. The idea is that in these ponds the oxygen drops and so how do the fish live there? Only those that can live in hypoxia will be there, but what species are they? And how do they do it?

What if I come, too? I ask him. There is room, he says, you should get a yellow fever shot. Sure, I'll get a shot, I tell him. We leave at the end of June, says Armando. Late June, Great, I tell him. Okay, see you later, I have to go to a lesson, Bye, Lapo!

I didn't have time to tell him I'd visit him for a year. I'll tell him via email. While I am there writing, someone knocks on the door and without saying anything, the secretary comes in.

So are you back? Yep, I tell her. Well, well, she tells me, there are a lot of things you have to sign. Don't think you're getting away with it. I can't wait, I tell her.

Here comes Malvezzi, he must have heard something, so there he is. Lapo, so you're back? It looks like it, I tell him. I'll tell Schifano right away, so that we can talk about the project, let's hope they approve it, he said. Right, I tell him, let's hope so. So, what's up with you, huh? What do think is up, I've been in a hospital for four months. What about your legs? Can you walk? Can you show me? I'm still not walking, I'm using crutches. And the nurses, huh, what were the nurses like? Pretty good, I tell him, they were pretty good. And Caterina comes to mind, now that I am leaving, I will never see her again. Although, I may still be able to see her at the day hospital. I could let her know that I'm leaving and she could come to the airport like in American movies.

In the meantime, Malvezzi stands there as he always does, and talks about this and that, while I write to Armando without looking up from the computer. There's this new guy, you know, Malvezzi tells me. He's an oceanographer, Baroni, he thinks he's so special because he makes very complicated mathematical models. He'll show you all these graphs with colors, etcetera etcetera, and then he says a lot of technical things just to confuse you. Schifano says it's a bunch of bullshit, I think he's a bit jealous, Schifano, because no one's paying attention to him, huh, what do you say? I don't know, I tell him, I don't know.

He's still there, Malvezzi, and doesn't leave. There's no way to get him out of here. He keeps talking, now he's talking about his son who plays wing on a local junior soccer team. When he sees that talking about work doesn't help, he shifts to soccer. He goes on and on, from his son's goals to soccer trades. Did you know that we may sign up Ganso? Who? Ganso, that Brazilian player . . . Uh-huh, I tell him, good idea. And what about you guys, who are you going to sign up? I actually think you need a new coach, don't you think? I don't know Corrado, I haven't paid attention to soccer lately, I tell him, I don't even know who won the championship. We did! We won it! Well done, I tell him, sorry now I have to make a phone call.

Finally he leaves, while I dial a random phone number. I hear a voice on the other line, but I don't hang up because I see Malvezzi turning around at the last moment, when he was almost out the door. How 'bout some coffee? No, thanks Corrado, thank you, see you later, I tell him, while I hear Hello? Hello? on the phone. I'm sorry, I've got the wrong number, I say, as soon as Malvezzi leaves.

The day goes by without any other incidents. Armando replies that I can stay in his lab for a year if I want. But if I want to go with him to the Pantanal, I have to get to Campo Grande by the end of June, because we will start from there, with his Jeep. I'd really like to go to the Pantanal, Armando often talks about it like a place out of this world. He says that it's full of anacondas, not to mention the caimans. According to Armando, in the Pantanal you can basically walk on caimans given how many there are. Along the banks of the Miranda river, capybara, rodents as big as wild boars, and jaguars come to drink. In the morning you wake up to the sound of howling monkeys and *cara cara*, birds of prey that are everywhere, he adds, you will see, you'll love the Pantanal.

Except for seeing Malvezzi another couple of times, and the secretary, and three other colleagues, including Schifano who, however, doesn't talk much, I luckily don't see anyone else. At six I go to catch the bus and go home. Then I call for a pizza delivery. Tomorrow I start physiotherapy in day hospital. I have to see if they'll let me go in late June. There are six weeks left, I may be able to make it.

Then I decide to call Uncle Beppe, so at least my mother would be happy. Whenever I call him, he always keeps me on the phone for half an hour, but on the other hand I'm at home, the house is half-empty, there is nothing to do, I don't feel like doing anything, except making it to the end of June. I call him. Hello? Who is it? Lapo, Uncle Beppe, this is Lapo, Marina's son . . . Hi Lapo! Lapone! or rather Lapino, or even better Lupin, when you were a child, I used to call you Lupin, Lupin, how are you, huh? I used to call you Lupin do you know what lupins are? And where are you calling me from, Lapo, do you have your own telephonation? Yes, I tell him. Good boy! So now you're a real man, in the olden days there were other things that would make you a real man, now it's the telephonation and all that new crap that works with waves or even the cars, now they're som'thin else . . . Y'know Lella just bought me a Japanese car, I dunno, a Toyota or a Mitsu-something or other or whatever Japanese car, it's got a dashyboardy that looks like a spaceship, geez, but she's the one who drives it, 'cuz I, let's not even talk about it, I just got out of da knife, I was under da knife, y'know, they kept me six hours, under da knife, like I was steaks, for Crissakes! Hey, y'know I've got lots of gifties for you, I'll send them to you, gimme your address, how 'bout this, send it to me via enails, do you have enails? Do you understand, do you use enails? Enails to send messages, do you have them? Then use them to send me messages, with enails . . . Guess what, for my enail address I had to use BAR instead of my name, can you believe that? BAR! BAR, like Beppe Alberto Rubatti, do you know why? Because there was another Beppe Rubatti, some guy from Bietrasanda . . . Dhey dalk lighe dis, lighe widh bickled jerries, this other Beppe guy had my same name so I had to come up with this acronym, can you believe it? All these things make me go purplish, you know what color I'm talking about, purplish, that's the color I am now, purplish, but why am I telling you this? Well it doesn't matter, so when are you coming for a visit? I've got lots of gifties to give you, y'know, I made some gizmos that you pull and they open or you let go and they close, they're funky little boxes, I'll keep them aside for you, you can put whatever you want in them, huh, now I have to say goodbye, Lella is calling me, okay Lapo, send me a buzz, hey, and now I'm saying goodbye, y'know, like they say on television, you know the *telefunken*? Those guys that are always there on TV, they're there and they stare at nothing and say *And thank you for the kind attention*, here I am telling you *And thank you for the kind attention,* but then you'll come and see me, I have lots of little gifties for you and also for Karin, say hello to her from me, okay? Of course, Uncle Beppe, I'll tell her. See you soon then and *thank you for your kind attention!*

I went to the day hospital this morning

I went to the day hospital this morning. Guglielmo found me in good shape so I asked him what he thought of the fact that I would go on a trip in late June. He told me that it's still too early to say, and that anyway if I want to go I have to sign some kind of release, and also that it's better if I find someone to take care of me wherever I have to go. I didn't tell him I'm going to

Brazil, I don't know why, but I just told him I am leaving. But I kept Brazil to myself.

Caterina did not show up. She doesn't work in day hospital but I thought that maybe she would come to visit me, but no.

Then in the afternoon I went back to work and continued with my hiding strategy. In fact, I didn't see almost anyone, except for Malvezzi from afar as I left my office to go to the bathroom where I stayed locked in for half an hour to increase the probability that Malvezzi wasn't just standing out there waiting for me. Fortunately, it worked. Then I called the chamber of commerce to inquire about the transportation of material abroad. Armando told me that he would like me to bring the high-speed video camera with me to film the movements of the fish. He told me that if I don't want to have problems with customs, I have to bring a booklet that shows that all the material I carry with me is going to come back to Italy. I asked around and it turns out that the Chamber of Commerce deals with these things. On the phone, they didn't seem to know what I was talking about, and they said, It's better if you come here in person to talk to the manager.

At the chamber of commerce

At the chamber of commerce they walk me to a huge office that looks like a gym with equipment. I didn't think a chamber of commerce would look like that. It looks like another type of *chamber*. There is a little guy sitting bent over a desk, with thick glasses and a mustache. *Pala Dino* is written on his desk. We shake hands and he says good morning. I say, Good morning, I would need to make a carnet for the transport of material abroad, since eventually I will bring it back to Italy.

I understand, he says, an ATA carnet. Right, I tell him, an ATA carnet. Do you need it for a demonstration? he asked. No, I need it for work, that is, I'm going to visit a colleague and I will be there for a few months. I need this material for work, it's video cameras. So you don't need it for a demonstration, or some kind of demonstration? Not really, I tell him. So, let's see, wait a second, I'm going get an old carnet.

He flips through the stacks of papers on his desk, and finally pulls out a green dossier and says, Here is an ATA carnet, see, they used it . . . let's see it here, he says, *For demonstration of material abroad.* You don't need it for demonstration, he said, did you? No, it's not really a demonstration, I tell him. So let's see, how can we do it, then, here you go, you put your name here, then you write the reason for the trip, for example for a demonstration, as it says here, then you should . . . here we go . . . here . . . where is it? I thought it was here, wait, you should put a list of the material, I can't find it, yet it was here . . .

Pala Dino starts leafing through the whole ATA carnet while he's saying it was here, it was . . . I'm sure, just give me a minute while I check. In the end, he finds the right page and shows me, Here, see this is the list of materials. Okay, I tell him, I have the list of materials ready, there are two cameras, I tell him, and show him. Right, yes, but we must also, there should be insurance, I think, wait a second while I'm checking, but I'm pretty sure you need insurance as well, just wait, I'm going to call a colleague to ask him. He picks up the phone and asks, Stefano, hi, listen, listen, for an ATA carnet, the ones people use to take demonstration material abroad, do you remember if insurance is necessary? Right, okay then it is necessary. Yes, insurance. Fine then, alright, you're saying it's necessary, yes, the insurance. Then he turns to me and says, Then yes, there would be a need for insurance. And what should I do, is there a particular procedure for this insurance? Hmm, he tells me, you should contact an insurance company to get insurance. Actually, there's one nearby, I can call it for you in a minute.

But first you should print the ATA carnet with the list of your material, do you have a file with the list? I give him the file, then I help him print the details of the material on the sheets of the ATA carnet. It's not a simple thing, you have to put the words in the right boxes, he says, the boxes, these boxes are a little difficult to put words into, if you can help me. I give him a hand, and we print several sheets, but then the printer jams. This printer, I don't know, it always gives me problems, always, now I'm going to try to pull out the sheet that got stuck, here, he says, while he pulls out the wrinkled sheet, here. We'll just stretch it a bit and then insert it in the carnet.

In the end I find myself with a slightly crooked booklet, because of the various crumpled sheets that got stuck in the printer and that Pala Dino managed to save and insert into the booklet. Then, he says, we're almost done, a couple of signatures are missing, and the date, the date, let's put . . . what date are we going to put, today is June 10th, the date, so let's put this date, he says, let's put today's date, which is actually June 10th.

Fine then, everything is ready, he says, it'll be sixty euros. I pay him, he gives me a receipt, and then he says to me, now if you have time, you should go to the insurance office, meanwhile I can call them, you can go ahead, I can call them while you walk over to their office, I'm sure they will answer the phone, he tells me, you just go ahead, that will be faster. It's just around the corner, Italassi Assicurazioni, he says, you can't miss it.

At the insurance agency

At the insurance agency, a woman in her fifties opens the door for me. Behind her, there is a room with four desks scattered at the corners of the room where as many women are sitting, and a more central one where no one is sitting. The woman asks me what I need, I explain the matter of the ATA carnet to her, and she says, Wait a moment please. I sit on a bench that was at the entrance, while she goes to one of the desks and starts talking to one of the other women. Then this other woman, a woman in her thirties, gets up and comes to me and says, Mr. Pardini, please take a seat.

I follow her and I sit down. She pulls cards out of a fat folder. She moves her hands dexterously, so fast that I can't focus on her hands. While she is leafing through, I notice between the interstices of her desk that she has taken off her sandals and is scratching her right calf with her left foot. She isn't exactly scratching herself, she is massaging slowly, at a much slower pace than the one with which her hands go back and forth on the folders she is leafing through. I wonder how she can keep these two different rhythms of her front and rear limbs. It can't be that easy, unless there is a relationship between the two rhythms, of the four-to-one type, four wrist flexions per each foot massage. Could be. The foot in tension for the message shows a firm but at the same time reassuring bridge, like some kind of intimacy through the interstices of the desk.

We could almost be at her home, sitting on a sofa, leafing through a magazine called *Homely Things*, I would have the same feeling of chills that I have now, if I were next to her on the sofa, while she was massaging her leg with her foot, and leafing through the magazine *Homely Things*. Maybe now there is an even greater intimacy since we are facing each other, and not next to each other and so we can look straight at each other and not sideways. After massaging her calf, she puts her feet back on her sandals, but not in the sandals. She has tapered feet with manicured nails but not overdone, and her big toe is the same length as her middle toe. They are looking at me from under the desk, while her upper body is still busy with the forms. Then she points her toes to the floor, delicately, and I realize she is about to talk to me. She tells me, Great, I've found the forms, there will be a lot of signing to do though. Okay, I say, I will sign whatever there is to sign.

One by one, the insurer hands me the forms and I can see her hands more closely, while we take turns at leafing through the pages to be signed. We pass each other the sheets, leafing through them in the same erogenous points, I have chills all along my right arm which I am using for signing and also my left arm which is taking the sheets that the insurer passes me. Her hands are slightly tanned and move with a small flicker that betrays a little inexperience. Her nails are lightly varnished, long but not too long, only shyly elongated. Her feet in comparison don't have many inhibitions. I lower my eyes to check, and in fact they are there, tapered as always, and looking at me.

I'm sorry to make you sign all these sheets, she says, there are so many. No problem, I tell her, in fact there isn't a problem, I have lost track of time, have I been here for half an hour or a year? Is the insurer selling me insurance or showing me the furniture for the living room of her dreams? I sign, I savor her hands with every sheet that she passes me by the now imperceptible distance, she practically touches my hand while she shows me where I need to sign, her feet are always there looking at me, every now and then they move a few centimeters, pushed by impulses unknown to me.

Finally, the last sheet to sign, Here is the last one, she tells me, with a kind of farewell sigh. I mumble something but I don't know what to say, I say something about signing, which is not a problem, I like to sign I must have said, she smiles, takes the last sheet and then gives me a folder. This is your insurance, do you need anything else? No, I say, no thanks, but what did she mean, do you need anything else, what else? No thank you, thank you very much, I tell her, she offers me her hand and I shake it, then she walks me to the door, Goodbye Mr. Pardini, she says, Goodbye, I tell her.

I go out and walk to the car. The cell phone rings, it's the insurer telling me, Mr. Pardini? This is Eleonora, of Italassi Insurance, remember to bring me the letter of custody from your institution. Okay, I tell her, is a fax fine too? Sure, she says, it's fine, if you can't come in person, a fax is also fine. Okay, so I'll send you a fax.

Then it occurs to me that I could have gone back in person, instead of the fax, why did I tell her about the fax? She also told me, *if you can't come in person*, but why did I come up with the fax? Sometimes I come up with ideas that go totally against my will and then I can't course correct, it's as if someone sent me random impulses which I end up incorporating. But in the end I have to say that I don't mind all that much, because this phenomenon spares me from having to decide personally about everything that happens to me. Often I make up my mind based on these random impulses, everything is easier this way, and in the end I feel even freer. I'll send her a fax.

The days go by

The days go by, and I keep going to work, hiding from Malvezzi, calling the central offices in Rome to see what forms I need to have the director sign for a year's permission, talking on the phone with my mother, talking with Armando via Skype, and going to day hospital almost every day. My legs are getting better, now I can walk without crutches, even if I have them with me at all times, and every now and then I use them so as not to get tired.

Since I left the hospital, it feels like I'm living in an intermediate state that isn't easy to define. I feel a bit like those chemical compounds that, when transforming from one stable substance to another, go through an unstable intermediate compound. For as much as I was steady, stable, during the days I spent at the hospital, now that I am out, it's as if I were living in a temporary stage that cannot last for too long. As a matter of fact, I'm going to leave, it almost seems to me that I have already left and that everything I am doing these days is something that one could easily describe by using the past tense.

Not only am I about to leave, but I could just as easily go back to the hospital, if only they'd let me. The other day at the day hospital, besides Guglielmo, there was Caterina/Katia, who was wandering the halls, tiptoeing around on Dr. Scholl's clogs, and I got shivers. I would have liked to follow her on her zigzag paths between the rooms, but I was there in front of the elevator with Gustavo, who was taking me to the physiotherapy room downstairs. In that very moment I thought I wanted to stay there and looked at Guglielmo as if to ask him if he could help me stay, but he turned around and pressed the elevator button, while Caterina turned the corner for the last time.

Therefore it's easier to leave, even if things seem to have taken a turn for the worse, a turn that does not seem to be resolved, as if this country has become more and more like a country where someone like Denis, my Russian-facilitator friend, is needed. He would be able to get me out of this mess, where the offices in Rome weave some of the most intricate textures possible, in which every single one of my calls is passed from one office to another and then goes back to the first office I called, where they tell me, Is it you again? And where to my answer, when I say that actually what I would like to do seems to be quite complicated, they agree with me, they tell me, Of course, what you want to do is a very complicated affair.

And then occasionally, one of them, an administrator with whom I speak, tells me that he or she will work it out, that he or she knows how to help me, I was really lucky to stumble upon him or her. And after explaining which forms I should download from the net, it always turns out that what they had in mind does not apply to my case, I didn't explain myself well, and then they give me another number.

And then my mother, she keeps calling me almost every day, asking me how I'm doing, and if I tell her that I'm improving, she tells me Hmmm, because she knows I want to leave, and therefore she says Hmmm, so I tell her, Look, I can even walk without crutches now, and she goes, Yes, but one thing is walking here on the streets, another is doing it in the middle of the jungle.

Unbelievable!

Unbelievable! I can finally leave! Everything turned out for the best, like when the roulette ball spins around and around, before choosing a number, and so I spun, between Guglielmo who said *take it easy* and the forms for the permits that could not be found, and when I did finally find them, the director who wouldn't sign them, Malvezzi who was asking me, But why are you leaving right now since you just got back? My mother who was asking me, But why are you leaving if you are not walking well yet, the ball was spinning round and round among all these things, and then suddenly it stopped on the right number, that is, on my departure. Gustavo said to me, It's okay, if you feel up to it, you can leave, the director suddenly signed what he was supposed to sign, and Malvezzi and my mother also got used to the idea of my departure.

Now I can walk with my own two legs, no more crutches, I have put them away. I talked to Armando to tell him that I can leave now, I started looking for flights, I told him, there is a daily flight to Sao Paulo, and in the end I bought a nice direct Rome-Sao Paulo ticket, I'm leaving in two days. Armando is waiting for me there, two more flights and we'll be in Campo Grande, then we take the jeep to go to the Pantanal. I already made a list of things to bring months ago, it's the thirty-eight objects on that list that I made while in the hospital, plus the two cameras. I also got the yellow fever shot, and I bought the pills for malaria, not the ones that give you nightmares, like when you are under the impression that everybody wants to throw you to the caimans, as Armando told me, but the almost harmless ones, except that they cost a fortune.

Meanwhile, I have emptied the house. I took all the books to Karin's friend at the library as a donation. Then I had a lot of pictures that I wanted to throw away, but my mother found out from Karin, and so she said she wanted them, and I gave them to her. I gave Marco most of my clothes. He told me he didn't need any more clothes, but that if I wanted, he would put them in the garage. The garage is fine, I told him, but it's fine to give them away too. And then I didn't even have to cancel the rent, because Karin told me she's going to live there again, now that I'm leaving. She didn't say she'd come back to live there because I'm leaving, she only said, Then I'll go back there, so when you come back from Brazil, I'll be there. I don't know what she meant, also because I would like to spend at least a year in Brazil, but maybe even more.

Yesterday was Luisa's birthday, and so it was also an opportunity to say goodbye to the whole family. They were all there, my mother, my brothers, even Karin, and also Uncle Beppe. Uncle Beppe started to make the capercaillie whistle, as he calls it, fufffiiii fuffiiii he went, covering his mouth with his hands like a trumpet, to blow my own horn, he said, Lapo! Fuffiiii fuffiiii, Lapo! Hey, watch out for the elephants!!

Marco and Simone gave me the usual fraternal pat on the back, also to check if I was falling down, I guess. Meanwhile, my mother was going on and on about being careful not to catch malaria, and watch out for typhus and yellow fever, and tetanus, did you get the tetanus shot? Yes Mom, I did that too, I told her. And cholera, did you get the cholera shot? No Mom, I didn't do that. And so? What if you get cholera? No, c'mon, I'll be careful, I won't get it. And now what are you going to do? Be careful with what you eat! Yes Mom, I'll be careful.

My mom went on and on for a while about the cholera. Then Luisa came and hugged me. Uncle Lapo! Uncle Lapo! When are you leaving? In two days, I told her. And when will you be back? In a little while, I told her, I didn't dare tell her *in a year*. Will you send me an email from Brazil? You know that now I have an email address, my dad did it for me, if you want I will write it on a piece of paper, she said.

Of course, I'll send you a message, I told her, and she gave me her email address. That way you can tell me about all the animals you see, okay, Uncle Lapo? Of course, I tell her. Are you going to send me some photos? Of course Luisa, I'll send you some photos, I tell her. Speaking of email, I also sent a message to my father to tell him that I'm going to Brazil, and as soon as I can, I will come to visit you in Buenos Aires, I told him. He replied almost immediately, he wrote to me, Okay, let me know when you arrive, that is, as many as seven words.

I got home at around one in the morning, the party went on for quite a bit, at some point Marco pulled out old photos of when we were children, and we looked at them until late. When I got home, I started putting things in my backpack, and I realized that I was putting everything I had left, I didn't even have to choose what to carry with me, I just put in the backpack all I have, and what I have is the list of the thirty-eight objects I thought of when I was in the hospital. And if I leave *Oblomov* and *A Man Asleep* here, the total goes down to thirty-six.

I put the two books on the table, next to a message for Karin—Please take these books to the library, thank you, Lapo.

Then I went to check all my documents, the ATA carnet, my passport, and I made sure my ticket was okay, I leave Rome at 10PM, and arrive in Sao Paulo at 5AM the next morning. It came to my mind that the world is small these days—with an ultra-modern plane you can find yourself on the other side of the earth in a dozen hours—and that this must mean something, but I'm not sure what. My father would probably say that if someone knows how to travel, even a paper plane is enough.

Dear Luisa

Dear Luisa,

How are you? Are you going to the beach these days? Here it must be about around nine o'clock, I guess, and we are going to bed, after a full day in the Pantanal. In fact, now that I see the clock, it's half past six in the afternoon on the third day since I got here. I am losing the sense of time, time has got its own pace here in the forest. In the morning around five o'clock the howling monkeys wake us up, there is no way to sleep here in the morning, so we go to bed earlier and earlier. Anyway, let's go in order, I'll tell you a little about what I've done so far and the animals I've seen, I'm also sending you some photos attached.

After arriving in Sao Paulo, go figure, I had to take three more planes to get to the southern part of Mato Grosso. My friend Armando was waiting for me and he took me to the middle of the Pantanal with a four-hour trip in the jeep. It was night when we arrived at this kind of ranch where we are sleeping. The ranch is next to a branch of the Rio Miranda. The next day, we went along the Rio Miranda by boat, a kind of Amazonian felucca, looking for caimans and jaguars.

This is how it works, Armando told me, if you see red eyes in the distance, it's caimans, if instead you see green eyes, it's jaguars. After a few minutes, we found ourselves surrounded by red eyes. They say that caimans don't jump out of the water to get on feluccas, at least not usually, according to Armando, so we took a lot of photos that I'm sending you. Then we also saw capybaras, which are the largest rodents in the world, let's say as big as a pig and even a little bigger. I am sending you a photo with the capybara mom and dad and five little babies who were going to have a picnic on the beach.

You know what piranhas are, right? So, in the afternoon we went fishing for piranhas! For real! So, first we were standing on this rundown little pier. That's how you start fishing for yellow piranhas. Armando got one, Felipe, one of his students, got another one, I was mostly taking the pictures I'm sending you. After a while, Felipe said, Hey, this one must be really big! So everybody went to see what was going on, maybe the hook got stuck on something, said Armando. After about a minute during which Felipe was standing with his rod heavily bent by the weight of the catch in the water, a three-meter caiman came up! I'm sending you a picture!

Before dinner, we also went on scientific expedition number one. First, I need to explain to you that here in the Pantanal there is a major swamp, especially during the rainy season from November to April. In the summer, however, it doesn't rain, so the ponds remain isolated from the river. And in these isolated ponds a lot of fish get trapped, and slowly consume all the oxygen in the pool. Many of them survive, but how do they do it? Long story short, we went in search of a pond to put in an instrument that Armando brought with him (he doesn't go anywhere without it), a kind of cylinder half a meter long that measures oxygen and temperature in the water. We put it in the pond today, and then we'll go get it tomorrow. In the evening we got back to the boat in search of green eyes, as we had seen enough red eyes. But no success. At least there was a beautiful sunset, and then at some point we were invaded by hordes of bats chasing mosquitoes. I'm not sending you those photos because you'd just see black!

On the second day we went around in the jeep, looking for other ponds. We saw ponds with capybaras, and also ponds full of caimans and giant otters. Above all, we discovered a pond in which catfish make a sort of big splash to go back to the bottom right after they come to the surface to get some fresh air. It's as if they are afraid that someone is up there ready to catch them and eat them. So if they are on the bottom that's bad because there's little oxygen, but if they come up, they must hurry otherwise someone will eat them. For this reason, they go up and down like some crazy elevator. They also seem to be somewhat synchronized, as soon as one comes up, the others will follow, perhaps that's a way to confuse their predators?

Then in the evening we went back to Rio Miranda. Look carefully at photo number 14. What do you see? Fronds? Tropical plants? Look better. What do you see behind the leaves? A jaguar! That's right! I also made a video, which I am not sending you because it is 40 megabytes, if I sent it to you it would be like trying to put an elephant in the mailbox. A jaguar, as I was saying, a real one, like really wild, and we watched it from our felucca, about four meters away. If it wanted to, it could have jumped into the water, I guess, and in fact I later discovered that jaguars are not like cats, like I originally thought. Apparently, jaguars can go into the water without any problems and can swim better than me.

Now I have to say goodbye to you and send you a big hug, the light is being turned off in the hut, that's the sign that we have to go to sleep. Say hello to everyone and tell Grandma that I'm fine otherwise she'll get all worried.

Uncle Lapo

I'm in Buenos Aires

I'm in Buenos Aires. The Pantanal seems like a distant memory. I still wake up at five in the morning, but there are no howling monkeys out there, there is Buenos Aires traffic. Armando is still there with his students, I took a week off to visit my father.

I wrote my father a message a few days ago telling him that I would arrive in Buenos Aires in early October. He replied Okay. At the beginning of October Armando could not give me a ride to Campo Grande and so I changed my ticket and arrived in Buenos Aires on September 30th. I go to my father's house near San Telmo, I ring the bell. The door opens. I go up the stairs. A bearded man opens the door and says, Lapo? Yes, I say. I'm Uncle Dino, don't you recognize me? he tells me. Uncle Dino is one of my father's three brothers, I haven't seen him for more than ten years, he looks quite a bit older, but the beard is new, so I say, The beard . . . Oh yes, he says, now I have a beard, it's true, we haven't seen each other for a while.

Uncle Dino lets me in and tells me to sit at a table where a gourd of *mate* was resting with its bombilla, that is, a straw. Uncle Dino passes it to me. I stand there, gourd in my hand, bombilla in my mouth, and I start to sip the hot *mate*. I look at

Uncle Dino a bit better, he is wearing only a white ribbed tank top and a pair of beige shorts, on his feet he wears a pair of old sandals with the back buckle facing the front, so that every now and then he can slip them off to better scratch his calf. Tank top, shorts and sandals all looked like my father's things, worn just like my father wore them. Uncle Dino looks at me, and tells me, So how long has it been since we last saw each other, Lapo, huh? Ten years, what do you say? It must be at least ten years? I stand there, sip the *mate* and nod. I wonder where my father is, maybe he is in some other room waiting for me, but I don't say anything.

Uncle Dino doesn't say anything anymore either. He asks me to pass him the *mate*. I look for something else to do, but I can't find it. There is not even a magazine around, nothing, just a wooden table, and a gourd full of *mate* that we keep passing to each other. Once the water in the gourd is finished, Uncle Dino adds some more from a thermos. Not even the shadow of my father. I'm sure Uncle Dino knows I'm here to see my father, but he doesn't say anything. I could say something to him, but since he already knows, I don't see why I should ask him something he already knows. So we stay like that, passing the gourd to each other, and refilling it, which is what he, Uncle Dino, does, whenever the hot water in the gourd runs out. We go on like this for a good hour.

Then Uncle Dino tells me, You're looking for your father. It's not a question, so I don't answer him, I continue to sip the *mate*, luckily it was my turn. He thought you would come in early October. It's true, yes, I told him so, but I had to come earlier because I couldn't get a ride to the airport in Brazil in early October. But where is my father? He'll be back, Uncle Dino tells me, he'll be back, don't worry, he'll be back tomorrow evening, he went to Puerto Madryn for a couple of days by plane. To Puerto Madryn? I ask him. Yes, Puerto Madryn, near the Valdez Peninsula, that's where whales can be seen from the coast at this time of year, so your father went to see them.

I picture my father walking along the cliffs of the Valdez peninsula, the wind against him, the whales jumping out of the water, and he keeps walking without even realizing it. And you, I ask Uncle Dino, you didn't go to see the whales? I was there last year, once you see a whale you've seen them all, he replies, scratching his calf once again. And your father wanted to go alone, you know how he is, right? As far as knowing how he is, I think, I do know a little bit, but there are some things that escape me. Where did that woman my mother calls *the ugly woman with her double chin* go? Why didn't she go with him to see the whales? Uncle Dino seems to read my thoughts, and tells me, your father is a loner, he always has been, do you know that woman he came to Argentina with? Right, I tell him, thinking, and now what's up with that?

She never existed, that woman. Or rather, there was an ex-colleague of your father who helped him settle in Argentina, but nothing else. Your mother saw her once at the airport, and got the idea that your father had run away with her, but that wasn't it, your father was just tired of everything, he had to leave. He was very tired and wasn't doing well. He was also being treated here in Buenos Aires, maybe you don't know that, but he's much better now anyway. I mean, he even went to see the whales, that's a good sign.

Great, I think, in two minutes I understood a lot of things about my father, like when suddenly there are three or four pieces of a puzzle that you have been trying to do for days and days, and then magically, piece after piece, you manage to finish it. It all comes back now, my father speaking to me in monosyllables, him being absent minded, running away, and giving up everything. Now that you know all these things, don't say anything to your father, and neither to your mother, Uncle Dino tells me. Of course, Uncle Dino, I tell him, you can take that to the bank. You can spend the night here if you want, there is a sofa over there, your father will be back tomorrow. No thanks, I tell him, I have already booked a *hostal*. It isn't true, I haven't booked any *hostals*, but I don't feel like staying there to hear whatever else Uncle Dino has to tell me. He has explained many things to me, and that's fine, but I am not ready for more things, even though he probably has nothing more to tell me. And then I don't feel like spending the whole evening passing the *mate* back and forth with Uncle Dino.

As you wish, Lapo. Anyways, your father arrives tomorrow at the airport, not the one outside the city, the one in Palermo, you see which one I mean? Yes, I tell him, I will find it. He's arriving at five twenty in the afternoon; directly from Puerto Madryn. Thank you, I tell him, and I set the *mate* gourd that I had been holding in my hand on the table, I get up, take my backpack, and go out. Uncle Dino accompanies me to the door and tells me, So, I'll see you Lapo.

I find myself in the street. It's already evening, and I have to find a place to sleep. I see an Internet cafe, I go in and look for a *hostal* in San Telmo. Luckily, there is one close enough. At the entrance, it's full of cats. I ask if there is a room. The guy at the reception tells me no rooms. He has a Brazilian accent and vaguely resembles Armando. He could be his son. Beds? I ask him. Beds yes, in dorms of four or six. Fine with me, I tell him. He takes me to a sort of basement full of more cats. There is cat smell everywhere. He shows me my bed. Then he shows me the bathroom, cats there too. I drop my backpack on the bed and go back up with him. How many nights? he asks me. How many nights I don't know, so I tell him a couple. Then I sit at the *hostal* table. There is some fruit on the table, and the Brazilian guy gestures for me to take it. I take an apple. Sitting near me there is a man with a mustache who sips *mate*, and on the other side of the table a girl busy with her cell phone. The *mate* guy asks me, Where are you from? He also has a Brazilian accent. I'm Italian, I tell him. Oh, he replies, it's been a while since we've seen any Italians, right Felipe? Felipe is the guy at the front desk. True, he goes, not too many Italians, the last ones a couple of years ago.

The guy with the mustache hands me the *mate*. My stomach is already full of Uncle Dino's *mate*, but I can't refuse. They say that *mate* is not something you like or don't like, it's something you just drink. So Armando once told me, though he is Brazilian, but these guys are also all Brazilians, to be honest. I stay there sipping *mate* a little longer, then I get up and lie down on the bed. I start to imagine the scene, me at the airport, my father arriving at the arrivals, and me greeting him from far away, from behind the people who are crowding up to welcome those who arrive. He, my father, finally sees me, but then I can't imagine the rest.

I get up in the morning with a cat

I get up in the morning with a cat on my stomach and the traffic rumbling from outside. This cat thing is a bit odd. They stay here as if it were their home, not really in line with any sort of hygiene regulations. I go up to breakfast, breakfast was included. Fruit, Felipe says, fruit and *mate*. I eat a banana and an apple, and Felipe hands me a *mate* gourd. We don't have coffee. I got that, I think, but I don't drink it anyways. I wouldn't even drink *mate*, but I have to drink something. A couple of cats vibrate around me. Yesterday's guy is still there, in the same position, and also the girl, with her cell phone. It looks like they have never moved.

I go out and find myself in the middle of the stalls in the San Telmo market. Zigzagging among the people, I find a bus stop. With a couple of buses, I make it to the Plaza de Mayo. I would like to see if there are pigeons. There are pigeons, I even try to feed them. They do eat, but none of them wants to be grabbed and put on my arm, like in that black and white photo of my distant relative, which I had seen as a child.

Maybe the square in the photo wasn't Plaza de Mayo. Or maybe after so many years, the pigeons have stopped perching on people who feed them, maybe someone has mistreated them and they have become shyer. I think back at the passerine that flew into my hospital room. Passerines can fly into rooms, but apparently pigeons don't do much, they don't jump on people's arms despite me having put some bread on my right arm. Nothing. They just wait for the bread to fall. In fact, at some point the bread falls on the ground and then they take it.

There's no way to pick up a pigeon around here. The photo must have been an artfully made photomontage, not like those Photoshop tricks people use nowadays. With Photoshop, I could cover myself with pigeons from all sides, on my arms, my legs even on my head. But I am not interested in the virtual reality of virtual pigeons. I set the rest of the bread I brought on the ground, the bread that was supposed to induce the pigeons to do what they hadn't done. They might as well take my bread, I divide it into several pieces, I set it here and there, go ahead, take my bread and eat it.

I take several buses, slowly I approach the Palermo district, where the airport is located, right in front of the Rio de la Plata. I get there too early. It's four o'clock, my father will arrive in more than an hour. I start walking on the seafront. I see a park, *Parque de la Memoria*, that's what it's called. In the park, there are entire walls covered with the names of *desaparecidos*, they are organized by year, there is a huge wall for 1976, they go up to the early eighties, the walls of the eighties are a little smaller. I start reading some names. It is amazing how reading a simple name on a gray wall can be so evocative. There are only the names, and the age. Sometimes, for some women, it also says *embarasada*, pregnant.

I go back to the airport. My father's plane has landed. I stand behind the barriers, behind a crowd of people with signs waiting for other people coming from Puerto Madryn. I am half hidden, in fact my father doesn't see me when he arrives, nor does he look for me, he most likely didn't hear from Uncle Dino and therefore, he doesn't know that I have come to get him. He's wearing the Lieutenant Colombo raincoat, and pulls a small, gray, slightly shabby trolley. He heads for the exit, I follow him. Then he stops near a pole, rummages in his pockets, pulls out a pack of cigarettes and lights one. The wind that comes from the Rio de la Plata carries a whiff of smoke that envelops me.

Paolo Pergola is the author of *Passaggi—avventure di un autostoppista (Rides: The Adventures of a Hitchhiker)* (Exorma, 2013) and *Attraverso la finestra di Snell (Through Snell's Window)* (Italo Svevo Edizione, 2019). His work has appeared in several Italian literary magazines. He is a member of OPLEPO/Opificio di Letteratura Potenziale (Workshop of Potential Literature), Italy's equivalent of France's OULIPO. He lives in Tuscany and works as a zoologist.

BLANK PAGE BOOKS

are dedicated to the memory of Royce M. Becker,
who designed Sagging Meniscus books from 2015–2020.

They are:

IVÁN ARGÜELLES
THE BLANK PAGE

JESI BENDER
KINDERKRANKENHAUS

MARVIN COHEN
BOOBOO ROI
THE HARD LIFE OF A STONE, AND OTHER THOUGHTS

GRAHAM GUEST
HENRY'S CHAPEL

JOSHUA KORNREICH
CAVANAUGH
SHAKES BEAR IN THE DARK

STEPHEN MOLES
YOUR DARK MEANING, MOUSE

M.J. NICHOLLS
CONDEMNED TO CYMRU

PAOLO PERGOLA
RESET

BARDSLEY ROSENBRIDGE
SORRY, I BROKE YOUR PROMISE

CHRISTOPHER CARTER SANDERSON
THE SUPPORT VERSES

www.ingramcontent.com/pod-product-compliance
Lightning Source LLC
Chambersburg PA
CBHW020023030726
47499CB00007B/2239